A [illegible]

Lord Richmond

Northcott Kinship Prequel

WENDY MAY ANDREWS

Sparrow Ink
www.sparrowink.com

ISBN - 978-1-989634-72-1

www.wendymayandrews.com

Stay in touch with Wendy May Andrews
and her upcoming publishing news.

Sign up for her biweekly newsletter

She'll *never* love him. Not again, anyway...

Lady Ellen Courtenay didn't think she'd see her first love again. After all, Hugh did kiss her sweetly, then abandon her without a backward glance. But that was years ago, and she plans to find and marry another. Her plan would've worked, too...if only she hadn't encountered Hugh at the ball and managed to somehow get herself involved in his investigation for the Crown...

Hugh never wanted to be anything but an agent. Sadly, the death of his father and brother left him no choice but to accept the title of Viscount Richmond and all the responsibilities that went with it. But before he can retire, he must finish one final assignment—all without giving in to his lingering attraction to the intelligent and tenacious Ellen...

When a case of mistaken identity forces Hugh and Ellen to fake courtship, will a little forced proximity and a *lot* of unresolved feelings earn them a second chance at happily ever after? Or will *Aiding Lord Richmond* only serve to break Ellen's heart yet again?

Get ready to swoon over this sweet regency romance. The romance is light and clean featuring a smart, strong heroine and the brooding hero who steals her heart.

Chapter One

The first ball of the Season, 1796

"Lady Eleanor Courtenay and her mother, Lady Hanley."

Ellen nearly tripped down the stairs when she heard how the majordomo had announced them. It was sheer effort of will that kept a smile on her face as she descended the stairs looking out over the sea of people milling about in the large ballroom.

A million thoughts raced through her mind even as she fought to keep a grimace from her face when she reached the crowds below with her mother at her side. It wasn't quite as she had expected. No one had warned her that it might not be the most pleasant smelling environment she had ever been in. It wasn't dreadful, of course, but in her many imaginings, somehow she had expected it to smell fresh and clean, perhaps like citrus fruit, which was an even more ridiculous thought than the rest that had preceded it. But the ridiculous thought helped her not make a cake of herself over the way she had been announced.

It was just that she had been so excited about making her debut. Having trained and practiced all the dance steps to every possible dance since before she could toddle, she had been very much looking forward to doing so at a real, proper ball. She and her mother had poured over fashion plates for hours deciding on what she ought to wear. Besides the practical aspects of making her debut, Ellen had also learned to draw, and paint, and perform all the possible needlework that a noblewoman could be required to do, besides how to plan a menu and run a household.

But in all her preparations, she had given no thought to how she would be announced. And now, what everyone she met was going to call her. A shudder made its way through her at the very thought. Eleanor. How grotesque. She had only ever been called that when her governess had been especially cross with her or if one of her sisters was trying to be particularly beastly. Ellen wondered what in the name of all that was holy her parents were thinking when they had settled upon that name for their newborn daughter.

Of course, it was to appease some long dead relative, Ellen was certain. But that didn't do her any good. Now she was going to have to grin and bear it, though she wasn't sure if she could. The very thought curdled her stomach.

"Stop frowning," Mama insisted from her side even while maintaining her own smile.

"How could you have told them my name was Eleanor?"

There was the briefest pause. "Well, that *is* your name." Mama's tone was that one of reasonable patience that only a mother could adopt. Ellen reminded herself that growling would be less than lady-like. It was also time to remind herself that while it might be Mama's fault she had such a dreadful name, it wasn't her fault that Ellen hated it so very much.

Eleanor might have been the name her parents had been so misguided as to appoint her with upon her birth, but no one actually ever called her that. She was

Ellen with friends and family alike. And it hadn't even crossed Ellen's mind to consider that Society might not know that.

It was mortifying. Was she to be Eleanor now for the rest of her life? If all these new acquaintances became a part of her future life, they wouldn't know that she loathed the name. How horrid. And how short sighted that she hadn't anticipated this. With the amount of thought and planning that had been put into making her debut, she should have seen this coming.

Ellen hated to be caught by surprise. She wanted all her surprises to be well planned out. And she couldn't give a fig if that was contradictory. It was how she felt, and there was no persuading her otherwise.

Now there was a gentleman bowing over her hand and being introduced to her.

"Good evening, Lady Eleanor, it is a pleasure to make your acquaintance."

Ellen wanted to throw a very uncharacteristic tantrum to vent the feelings welling up within herself. But of course, she couldn't do that. She was well aware that she was being ridiculous, but her feelings were her feelings even if no one could quite sympathize with them. Instead of giving way to her contrary emotions, she smiled at the man. She had been far too upset to catch his name. She rather thought it had been mister something. Not lord. That might suit her just fine, she thought.

What an odd conundrum. To be assessing each gentleman she met as a possible husband. Did she want to marry a lord? She should have given that more thought.

Ellen had thought she had prepared well for her Season. It would now seem that she hadn't considered any of the most important factors. But then she was being swept into the flow of her first dance at her first ball of her first Season, and she was able to leave those concerns to the side for the time being.

Really her first dance ought to have been with her father or her brother. But Lord Hanley and Baron Hastings had both remained behind at Hanley House to deal with a problem with one of their herds. Her father, the Earl of Hanley, dearly loved to take his Seat in the House. It had been a surprise to all in the family when he had allowed his wife and daughter to travel up to Town without him. And so, here Ellen was taking her first dance with someone whose name she couldn't even recall.

She refused to consider it a disaster, though, reminding herself of her determination to have a brilliant Season. She might not be a Diamond of the First Waters, but Ellen knew she was acceptably pretty. That, accompanied by the fact that she had a reasonable dowry, would ensure that she ought to be a success. If anyone could forgive the fact that she had been saddled with the unfortunate name of Eleanor and she was dressed in the most casual of current fashion, that was.

That was one more point of disfavor for this rather inauspicious start to her debut. It had been a massive disappointment for her that hoops and panniers were no longer the fashion, but she had to admit the style of gowns that were now popular were far more comfortable than those previous styles would have been.

She couldn't accept that the current styles were more elegant. To Ellen's mind they seemed almost like nightrails. As she glanced around at the other ladies, she was not disabused of this thought. Very much more comfortable than navigating a hoop through a crowded ballroom, but far too casual to be called elegant in her mind. But her older sister had assured her that she wasn't violating any Society standards by adopting the new styles. In fact, Theodora had assured her, if she turned up anywhere but the queen's drawing room in the old styles, she would be ridiculed all the way back to their village. And so, Ellen had accepted the styles and had ordered the gowns and had practiced the steps and done all the things a young lady could do to prepare for her first Season. And yet it was a great big flop.

Pasting a smile to her lips, Ellen reprimanded herself for being a ninny. She couldn't throw away the delight of her first official ball as a debutante by lamenting what might have been.

Despite her unfortunate name, this nice gentleman had asked her to dance. She ought to be making the most of the opportunity.

"I apologize, but I did not catch from where you hail." She rather thought that was a brilliant way of trying to figure out who he might be.

The gentleman smiled kindly at her. "Cornwall, my lady."

Ellen's lips twitched. That wasn't the least bit informative since Cornwall encompassed nearly a quarter of the country.

"Have you been in Town long?"

She thought of asking if he took a Seat in the House but if he was a mister as she suspected, that wasn't terribly likely unless he was someone's proxy. But then he surprised her by being a trifle more informative.

"I am clerking for the Earl of Sunderland, so I came to Town with him just before the opening of the current Session. We were surprised not to see your father. I do hope he is well."

"Oh yes, quite well. He should be in attendance quite soon. There was some trouble on the estate he had to attend to, but he and Jeffrey should be along within the next fortnight."

"It must be terrible trouble for Lord Hanley to not take his Seat."

Ellen felt heat growing in her chest. She had perhaps been an inconsiderate beast. She hadn't given thought to how out of character it was for her father to remain at home when Parliament was in session. It was true, never in her life had it happened before. It had actually been a point of contention within the family that he had never missed a sitting. He had missed plenty of other things – family things – but never a sitting of the House. Ellen bit her lip. She ought to have asked more questions.

Somehow she managed to get through the dance. Ellen was reasonably sure that she smiled and nodded and made appropriate sounds in all the right places. She had been raised for this moment and knew what to do almost instinctively. But her mind and heart were elsewhere. She only hoped it wasn't terribly evident to the gentleman and that she caused no offense.

She must have done a semblance of a good job going through the motions of social niceties or else he was the most kind and charming fellow, and she was even more of a beast for not having paid him more mind. He didn't seem to have noticed or he hid it well as he bowed over her hand and thanked her quite handsomely for the dance when he delivered her back to her mother's side at the end of it.

"Are you unwell?" Mama's question wasn't as solicitous as the words implied. She kept her voice low, but her fury was clear to be heard, leading Ellen to suspect that she hadn't hidden her inattention from her mother, at least.

"Quite well, thank you, Mama." She hoped her mother wouldn't pursue her irritation any further. "I have a question. Ought we to have remained at Hanley to assist Father in whatever is wrong with the flock? It has been remarked upon how very unlikely it is for him to be late to Parliament."

To Ellen's dismay, she felt the clog of tears welling in her throat, and she swallowed it down forcefully. It would certainly not do her any favours to be seen bursting into tears in her first ballroom. She pinned a practiced smile to her face even as she awaited her mother's reply. Despite being the youngest child, Ellen had never considered herself to be spoiled and hated to think she had been selfish in coming to Town without her father and brother.

"Do not be more ridiculous than necessary, my dear. Of course, we shouldn't have stayed at home. Of what use do you think you or I could be to the poor sheep?"

Ellen blinked and then grinned. She couldn't really fault her mother's reasoning. Before she could think of another way to ask her concerns, their hostess was bringing another gentleman to introduce to her, and she was again swept out onto the dance floor.

In between dances with what felt like dozens of eligible gentlemen, Ellen also had the opportunity to meet several of her fellow debutantes. The gentlemen were all varying degrees of pleasant and kind, even if they weren't all exceedingly enthusiastic about meeting her. Those less delighted to make her acquaintance seemed to be gentlemen determined to maintain their single status. It amused Ellen to no end. Less amusing were some of the ladies she met. Ellen couldn't have explained quite why she found the women more alarming than the men; perhaps it was her own knowledge of her sisters and what it would mean if their faces held just such an expression.

One such introduction was to Lady Constance. She and her mother curtsied politely to Ellen and her mother. Ellen had the impression Lady Hanley was already acquainted with Lady Constance's mother, Viscountess Moore, but they didn't appear overly friendly. That too put Ellen on edge even without taking into consideration the other debutante's perfectly arranged tight curls that appeared to be defying gravity in the artful arrangement they had been placed in. Ellen refused to allow her hand to lift to ensure her own were remaining where they ought to be.

Having curtsied and exchanged pleasantries for a few seemingly unproductive minutes, Ellen wasn't disappointed when the interlude came to an end as Constance and Ellen were both claimed for the next dance.

The evening was flying by. Despite the dilemma of being constantly addressed as Lady Eleanor, and besides the concern niggling at the back of her mind about her father's absence, Ellen was managing to have an excellent time. She was having a successful start to her Season indeed. What a relief.

"Lady Eleanor? How strange." The smirk on the face of the man currently bowing over her hand let Ellen know that he was teasing her and not actually saying that she was strange.

In an effort to curb the conflicted feelings that engulfed her at her first sight in four years of the man who stole her heart, Ellen widened her polite smile into one she hoped appeared genuine. Hugh Turner. Or rather, Lord Richmond, had always been the most handsome man she'd clapped eyes upon. But she couldn't allow herself to become tongue tied no matter how well he looked. She might not appreciate the latest female fashions, but the men's fashions certainly suited the viscount in front of her.

"Isn't it though? Who'd have thought they would be so foolish as to announce me by the name given me at birth." She knew the wide grin she was offering to him was making her silly dimples show, but she couldn't seem to stop her instinctive reaction to her seeing her brother's friend. "How are you, Hugh? Or rather, I suppose I ought to call you Lord Richmond now, shouldn't I? I was so sorry to hear about your father and brother. I never knew your father, but I couldn't believe Peter would ever be caught in a boating accident. How are you holding up?"

His face was tight, but he nodded and smiled a little before he bowed gallantly over her hand with an elegant flourish that rather belied the serious moment.

"Thank you, my lady, I am well." He quickly turned the subject. "Where is Jeffrey? I would think he'd be dancing attendance on you just as he did with Theodora. It was the most amusing thing in the world to watch your brother hover over his sister like a mother hen. Seeing you here, I was hoping for a good laugh at Jeffrey's expense."

"Actually," Ellen began, lowering her voice so he had to bend his head to hear her over the loud hum of the assembled crowds. "Could I talk to you about that?"

Hugh frowned. "Do you expect privacy? Because despite our long friendship, I do not think it would be considered acceptable for us to be seeking a private conversation."

Ellen flushed at his words but didn't retract her own. Never mind the effort it took to ignore the memory of a time when they had sought private conversation.

"Shall we dance? This next one sounds like it's to be a minuet. We should be able to exchange a few words without anyone paying a great deal of attention."

Ellen was relieved that he was going to speak with her. Despite his saying they'd had a long friendship, Ellen had never thought he considered her or her sisters anything but a terrible nuisance, except that one summer Ellen refused to think about. But it had been several years since she'd seen him, even though she knew Jeffrey kept in touch with all his old friends from school.

"Thank you, my lord," she said shyly as she stepped into his arms. It felt strange being in grown up Hugh's arms. She had, of course, danced with him when she was young. Jeffrey's friends had all been enlisted into helping their friend's three little sisters practice their steps. But Ellen was no longer a child, and Hugh was certainly a grown man.

Ellen couldn't have said why being in his arms felt any different than any of the other handsome men she had danced with that evening. Perhaps it was the air of familiarity between them, she thought. It certainly couldn't be that she found him any more attractive than any of the other gentlemen. Hugh was Jeffrey's friend. And he had just come into his title quite suddenly. Despite his presence in Town for the Season, surely he wasn't looking for a wife at this time. Was he even old enough? Ellen rather thought all of Jeffrey's friends wished to put off getting leg-shackled as they called it as long as humanly possible. And him in mourning besides.

She glanced at his black arm band. In fact, it was a little odd that he was even present that evening. Ellen couldn't remember the dates of their deaths, but surely Hugh ought to still be at home on his newly acquired estate. It had certainly not been a full six months yet. A frown started to form on her forehead.

"You had wished to speak with me?" he prodded. "I'm certain that wasn't some sorry attempt at making me dance with you."

The laughter dancing in his eyes along with their long knowledge of each other kept Ellen from getting angrier with him than his teasing warranted. Besides, he was right, she did wish to speak to him, and she shouldn't allow the strange sensations coursing through her to distract her from her intentions.

"Yes, thank you for the reminder. The thing is, I'm not sure if it's a delicate matter. Have you heard from Jeffrey?"

The strangest sensation trickled through Ellen as she observed no shift upon Hugh's face. He appeared completely pleasant and unconcerned, almost as though he hadn't even heard her question. It was an odd reaction on his part, considering she was certain there was a furrow of worry between her own eyebrows and she had thought she felt his hands tighten on her ever so slightly when she started speaking.

"I hear from Jeffrey fairly regularly," he answered mildly. "Your brother is an excellent correspondent. Quite remarkably so for a gentleman, in fact. I've heard that it's more a female activity to write to one's friends so often. But your brother can be found putting pen to paper nearly every day in order to maintain contact with his many friends."

Ellen pinched her lips between her teeth and lowered her eyebrows for the briefest moment before she heard the whisper of her mother's voice within her head reminding her that she shouldn't be frowning at a Society ball. That thought nearly made her laugh, and she found herself grinning again up into Hugh's surprised face.

Chapter Two

Hugh wasn't in Town to dance attendance upon his friend's little sister, he reminded himself even as he held her to him as closely as polite Society would permit. He really shouldn't even be out in Society. It was barely six months since his brother and father had died, making him the Viscount of Richmond. It wasn't a situation he ever thought to occupy and certainly not one he had wished for.

In fact, it was ruining his life.

But Ellen Courtenay couldn't possibly know that. And it was ridiculous for Hugh to be resenting her and her adorable dimples. Those dimples, he knew, were the bane of Ellen's existence. She usually contained herself to small, gentle smiles so they would not reveal themselves. It was actually probably a testament to their long acquaintance that she was allowing them out of hiding that evening.

He thought they were the most precious things he had seen in an age. Perhaps since the last time he had seen her dimples. It had been more than three years since he had visited his friend Jeffrey on his family's estate. So much had changed recently. The sight of those lovely crevices in her cheeks made him have need to admonish himself once more about the impropriety of his current situation. His mind turned again to what had brought him to this moment.

He had been on a mission in France when his brother and father had drowned in that sudden, monstrous boating accident. Hugh tried to tell himself it was pointless to be angry with them. *But why hadn't they brought servants with them?* It had been just the two of them out on the water in their small skiff that day when a squall had blown up and overwhelmed them. Or at least, that is what he had been told when the runners had finally found him in Paris where he had been stationed for some time.

It was hard to bear the disappointment in his mother's eyes when she thought he had been there drinking and wenching, rather than the real reason for his time in Paris. But he couldn't tell her why and had to allow her to think what she will. But that was why he was again in the great metropolis. He needed to hand over his responsibilities for his mission and leave off his role with the Home Office. He had to be the staid and responsible Viscount of Richmond now and take care of his mother as she saw fit.

Of course, Lady Richmond was quite determined to become the Dowager Viscountess and was diligently and unfortunately regularly expressing her feelings on the subject to her only remaining child.

Hugh was well aware that marrying and starting a family was part of the responsibility that came along with the title. And his father's and brother's deaths had well illustrated how unpredictable life could be, so Hugh knew he needed to think about finding himself a wife. But now was not the time. He already had to accept far too many changes in his life. Adding a wife into the mix was not going to simplify his life in any way. And until he got this matter sorted out, it might not actually even be safe to take a wife.

At least not for whichever young lady he happened to wed.

Not that he had any intention of wedding.

And especially not with Jeffrey's little sister, no matter how endearing her dimples might be. He dragged his thoughts away from his morose musings and tried to focus on what Ellen was saying without actually thinking about how very pretty she was with her curls all piled on top of her head and her pretty gown flowing on her clearly grown up form.

And now the pretty little thing was asking him something about her brother and appeared to be genuinely worried about something. As a gentleman, he couldn't really do nothing. Stifling the deep sigh he truly longed to utter, Hugh made an effort to be conciliatory.

"What exactly is the issue? Why did you ask if I've heard from him?"

The girl managed to shrug and follow his steps quite skillfully without missing a single step. And then she sighed.

"A gentleman I was dancing with expressed his immense surprise that my father hasn't come up to Town yet even though Parliament is in Session. I feel like a veritable beast as I didn't really think about it when Mama and I were finalizing our plans to come without him."

She sighed again and shook her head. "But that gentleman was quite correct. In all my life, Father has never missed the opening of Parliament. Even when Amelia was about to be born, he came up, much to Mama's displeasure. So it makes me think that the problems with the flock that kept them home must be far more serious than anyone is letting on, or perhaps it's even a ruse of some sort so as to not tell me the real reason." She smiled through her obvious worry. "I mean, really, Father isn't usually that involved with the flocks, as far as I've noticed. But perhaps I'm a selfish beast who pays no attention to such things, and he's actually always acting the shepherd." The girl sighed once more and then looked up at him quite trustingly, as though she expected him to answer every last question that might arise into her pretty little head.

Hugh felt his chest puff up in the strangest way. It was as though his subconscious thrilled at the thought of answering every one of her questions just exactly as she expected. He ignored the sensation no matter how surprisingly pleasurable it seemed. He couldn't deal with any other than his own issues in that moment.

"It does sound unlike Hanley to stay away. But I haven't heard anything that ought to trouble you from Jeffrey," Hugh found himself saying. "Would you like me to send a courier to find out?" He didn't know he was about to offer that until the words were already out of his mouth.

"Would you?" The delighted expression upon her face made him forget about his own chagrin.

"It's the simplest thing for me to do. I'd be happy to do it. As you know, Jeffrey is one of my oldest friends. I would hate to think of him and your father having a big issue on their hands." Suddenly he called himself to his senses. "But I'm sure it isn't anything for you to concern yourself over. As you said, surely if there was a real problem, they wouldn't have sent you to Town."

Her expressive face was a contradictory mix of pleased and doubtful. If Hugh had to guess her thoughts, he surmised that while she was delighted by his offer to send a courier, she wasn't certain of his reasoning on whether or not there was reason for her to be concerned about her home.

While Hugh had many other things to take care of, it really wasn't a large commitment to send a courier to Hanley House. He had a great number of them that must be quite bored now that he was leaving his life as an agent behind. They would be eager for even such a simple assignment. And now that he thought on it, it *was* a strange thing that neither Lord Hanley nor his son, Baron Hastings, were present for Lady Ellen's debut.

But of course, he couldn't allow the lady to worry.

"How are you enjoying your first Season?"

"Well, as you noted, it is decidedly strange to be meeting people as Lady Eleanor rather than Lady Ellen. But other than that, it has been delightful. Well, that and this concern that I have ignored a very obvious problem at home, so it makes me feel like the worst daughter ever born."

Hugh chuckled.

"You, my dear, are the furthest thing from the worst daughter, believe me."

"How would you know? You have no sisters or daughters."

Hugh smiled in response, not bothering to answer with words. He didn't have time for complications. And certainly not with this particular woman. Their history was complicated enough. He couldn't add to it by rekindling any old feelings.

The innocent young woman smiled up at him with the greatest faith as though he were jesting with her as a family friend rather than the hardened agent of the Crown that he truly was. Hugh's gut clenched. He supposed one day he might be able to be the noble gentleman she thought him. But today was not that day. After he danced with her, he would have to find the one he had come to the ball to speak with. He wanted to leave this crowded room full of sweet, innocent young people who still looked at the world through the protected lenses that people like him provided.

It was one more reason he was furious that he had to give up his work. All this innocence needed to be protected. Sweet young ladies like Lady Ellen didn't need to know that evil villains existed anywhere but between the pages of their favorite gothic novels.

What had his father and brother been thinking? He should never have been Viscount Richmond. Or Viscount of Richmond, he supposed. It was not a courtesy title. He had to bear all the responsibility for the large viscountcy.

And aside from the foolishness of taking the skiff out without sufficient help on a day that the weather could be sketchy, the true Viscount of Richmond, Hugh's father, had been a very responsible custodian of his own little empire. Hugh had inherited a great deal of wealth and property that he had absolutely no desire to take over. His brother was supposed to do it.

The only thing that made it remotely palatable for Hugh was the fact that as the spare who was never supposed to inherit, he had actually been given at least a modicum of training in the running of the estate, so he wasn't likely to run it completely into the ground in his first six months while he mourned all his losses, both his family members and the role he had loved.

He needed to find Gilbert Northcott. Perhaps if he were able to enlist his old friend into the role he hated to leave he would be able to let it go a little easier. Knowing his last mission was in capable hands would allow him to sleep a little easier at night, even if he still mourned. But as it stood now, he worried for the state and safety of the great nation he had sworn to serve. He couldn't concentrate on the viscountcy until he knew it was secure.

He bowed over the lady's hand and was about to take his leave of her when Ellen's small hand tightened on his.

"I'm sorry to bother you with this personal matter, Lord Richmond, but could I count on you to let me know what you learn from your courier?"

Hugh blinked at the chit. He hadn't thought that far ahead. He had never had such ties before. But there was nothing for it but to agree.

"Of course," he answered almost instantly. "How about I call around to take you for a drive in a couple of days? I should surely have news by then."

"Oh, how delightful that would be. It would feel almost homey. Thank you, Hugh, or rather, my lord." The girl blushed and stammered and suddenly looked just exactly like the young schoolgirl he remembered from his days of visiting her brother on school holidays. He had to admit, he was surprised she was being so pleasant to him. If he had thought it through, he would have expected her to be much cooler toward him, considering their last encounter.

Again he chose to ignore the pulse of something that he felt from viewing her in this light. He wasn't ready to have feelings. Especially those particular feelings. He had turned those off years ago and had no room for any feelings other than his anger and grief.

"I will call on you, then, as soon as I have any information for you. I'll bid you goodnight." The heat of her stare seemed to burn between his shoulder blades as he walked away, but he didn't dare look back to see whether or not her eyes upon him was just his imagination.

Hugh made a mental note to remember to send Johnny, his most trusted courier and one that Jeffrey would recognize, to check on the situation at Hanley House, but for now he pushed the matter to the back of his mind. He didn't have enough space in his thoughts to concern himself with it while he was also dealing with the matter of his worries for the Crown.

Chapter Three

It was a gloriously sunny day despite the cooler temperatures of late September. After having slept much later than usual, Ellen was now sitting at her *escritoire* contemplating the previous night, the cause of her sluggishness that morning. She had enjoyed her first official ball quite immensely, and she had felt like a success. Surely it wasn't terribly conceited of her to think so. She hadn't been the most popular girl at the ball, but she also hadn't spent any time on the sidelines. For that, she was deeply grateful. It was Ellen's strong opinion that either circumstance would be dreadful in the extreme.

But while it had been a highly enjoyable night, Ellen was determined to find her match that Season and get on with life. She knew some young ladies wanted to just play at courtships for their first Season and then get serious about marriage during their second or third Season. Ellen wasn't one of those.

It wasn't as though she were in competition with her sisters, but Theodora had married within weeks of her debut and was now well ensconced in her life with her husband and baby. And Ellen's younger sister, Amelia, would be hoping to make her debut in a couple years. Ellen loved both her sisters immensely, but she didn't think she would wish to share a Season with either of them. Then perhaps it *would* feel like a competition, and she had no interest in experiencing that. No, Ellen needed to be serious about matters. She wasn't in Town to make merry. She too wanted to be well settled into her new life before Amelia made her debut.

And so, she was sitting at her letter writing desk, quill in hand, tapping her finger against her chin, deep in thought over the night before. She didn't think it especially *gauche* to make a list of anyone she had met the night before who might be considered an eligible *parti*. This was the point of her being there, and how else was she to consider her options if not to write it all down?

Mr. Browne

Mr. Gilbert Northcott

Lord Richmond

Ellen tapped her chin again. Perhaps not Lord Richmond. As the new Viscount of Richmond, Ellen was quite sure Hugh was far too preoccupied to consider matrimony at this time. And she couldn't wait around for him, no matter the delicious shivers that were produced when he had chuckled over something she had said. The way his face had lightened when he'd laughed had made her feel as though she had accomplished something great. Clearly the poor man had experienced far too little laughter in recent times.

Besides the fact that he was obviously not yet in a position to pursue matrimony, there was also that old matter between them. No, she drew a line through his name on her list. He was not a potential for her.

Turning her mind away from Hugh, Ellen thought about the other gentlemen on her list. She didn't know much about Mr. Browne. Not even his first name, which was rather short-sighted of her and just went to show how distracted she had been early in the evening. He had seemed quite pleasant and had shown marked interest in her, listening attentively when she'd spoken rather than looking around the room as some others had done. She would do well to find out a little more about his circumstances and get to know him a little better.

Then there was Mr. Gilbert Northcott. As the second son of the Earl of Everleigh, he wasn't a peer and wasn't likely to ever be one. Although Hugh's situation just went to show that anything could happen. But there were rumors that Mr. Northcott did have property of his own with sufficient living that he was an eligible bachelor. Ellen didn't much care about titles. She had already been a lady all her life. She wouldn't miss it terribly if she were to marry an honorable instead.

Mr. Northcott had been pleasant and personable and was an excellent dancer. And there had been none of those confusing shivers when he had pressed his lips to the back of her hand. He might do quite nicely for her, she thought with a nod. But she needn't make up her mind after her first ball, she assured herself. Besides, none of the gentlemen had even called on her yet, so she ought not get ahead of herself. She would keep her list and perhaps add to it in time.

Just as she put away her quill, a maid was at her door to tell her she had a visitor. Lady Constance? Why would she be calling? Ellen quickly checked her appearance in the mirror. She hadn't paid too much attention to her toilette that morning. Were her curls all where they ought to be? She frowned over her imperfections but refused to allow herself to be intimidated by the pretty visitor before following the maid from the room.

Lady Constance was waiting for her in the front receiving room with a maid waiting with her. She and Ellen had been introduced the night before, but Ellen hadn't gained the impression that her visitor had been all that friendly toward her. In fact, she had heard whispers of Lady Constance's penchant for gossip. This did not bode well. Curtsying, Ellen wondered and worried why the woman was there.

"I do hope you don't mind my tuning up unannounced," the girl began in an earnest manner. "I forgot that I was supposed to ask you when you are at home to visitors. But I thought I'd take a chance and see if you might be available to go strolling in the Park with me."

"Oh, what a singularly good idea," Ellen exclaimed, fighting the urge to clap her hands as she reminded herself that she was a mature young lady of Society now. "It is one of the things I miss the most being away from home. I would love to go for a walk with you." She stopped for a moment and pulled a face. "My apologies, my lady. Ought I to have offered you some refreshments first?"

The guest uttered a small tinkle of laughter. "Absolutely not. I have arrived unannounced, you needn't offer me anything. And truly, I would much rather go for a walk than anything else. Even though I danced quite a lot last night, I still feel restless. Or perhaps it is because I danced so much last night that my feet just cannot bear to be still today."

Surprised by the seeming friendliness of the other woman, Ellen couldn't help but agree. "How delightful, then," she said. "Let me just let my mother know. I shall then grab my spencer and my maid, and we can be on our way."

Within minutes the two young women were arm in arm, walking briskly through the crisp fall day. Their maids became acquainted and did their best to keep up.

"Now tell me, Lady Eleanor, what are your thoughts after your first ball? Are you thrilled to be here, or do you wish you could run home to Somerset?"

Ellen threw her head back and laughed at the question. "Are those my only choices? To be honest, I cannot quite decide between the two. I feel a little bit of both. What about you? Did you love it?"

Lady Constance trilled a laugh and shook her curls, making a curdle of envy grow in Ellen's heart that she quickly tried to stifle. "I am one of those strange creatures who doesn't wish to wed right away. I am not in a hurry to trade my large dowry to become some gentleman's possession. I think this is the one time in my life when I will feel the most independent. I want to savour it for as long as I possibly can."

Ellen stared at her in wonder. "Do you truly feel independent? As a debutante, we must follow a myriad of rules, else we'll be ruined. Besides, I have absolutely no desire to tarry in this in between era of my life." Interrupting herself for a moment to curtsy to a couple she had met the night before, Ellen carried on as though there had been no pause. "Since it has been decided by my family that I am of the age to marry, I wish to get on with it. So while the idea of making such a monumental decision scares the life out of me, I have no desire to wallow in it." Realizing that perhaps she had just insulted the other woman, she hurried to turn the topic slightly. "And the thought of risking scandal makes me feel as though I shall break out in hives. So while a part of me wishes to change my mind and run home to Hanley House and remain a schoolgirl a while longer, I shan't. And only you and my maid need ever be privy to by momentary cowardice."

Another trill of laughter came from the pretty lady, making Ellen begin to wonder if she ought to have accepted her offer of friendship, but then Lady

Constance tightened her grip on Ellen's elbow as though to offer her an embrace. "You and I are going to be great friends, I am determined on it. So I do wish you would change your mind and join me in remaining a debutante for longer. If I cannot convince you to do that, I shall just have to ensure you wed a peer, and then you'll have to come up for the Season anyway so he can take his Seat."

Ellen wasn't too sure about the other woman's reasoning. While the ball last night had been delightful, she wasn't certain she wished to be a part of the social whirl on a regular basis. Just this visit with Lady Constance was revealing to her some of the pitfalls of the Season. Gossip and knowing who's who wasn't really to her taste. Well. Only one of the gentlemen currently on her list was a peer, and she had already been considering removing him from that list anyway. There was, of course, the untitled gentleman who clerked for Sunderland, but Ellen hadn't even written him onto her list because she thought a clerk's wife might not be to her taste either.

"Do you think the Season would be quite different if you weren't a debutante?" She could hear the tremulous tone in her voice and cringed but didn't retract her question.

"Indubitably."

Ellen stared straight ahead, not meeting her friend's gaze. Nodding to another pair they encountered upon the path.

"In what ways would it be different?" she asked after clearing her throat in order to put a little more strength into her voice.

"Well, for one thing, the decision would be over. You wouldn't be in the Marriage Mart. I would think it would be far more enjoyable. I intend to enjoy this Season, so it isn't the same for me. But for a serious girl like you who doesn't want to prolong the experience, you aren't really going to enjoy yourself to the full. As a wife, you won't be subject to all the rules and risks of scandal. And you can just pick and choose which entertainments you wish to accept rather than the ones most likely to land you an eligible bachelor."

Finally, Ellen laughed and relaxed in her new friend's company. "Very well, then. Let us search out a peer for me to set my cap at."

Horror filled her as the words left her mouth, as if she would even think of setting her cap at anyone. Even though she had happily made a list of eligible gentlemen, that was a far cry from actually beginning a pursuit. But she managed to keep her lips shut and didn't retract her words. She was almost certain Lady Constance would take them as the jest they had been intended, and making much over them would only make it worse. But it still filled Ellen with discomfort, and some of the shine had been removed from the day.

"What about Richmond?"

Ellen blinked. "What of him?" Suspicion filled her.

"He might be the perfect match for you." Lady Constance said it in a tone as though she were explaining it to a young child, making Ellen laugh despite not enjoying her condescension.

"I think it's too soon for him to be thinking to wed after losing both his brother and his father. Besides, he has been friends with my brother since they were young boys. That might be much too strange. He's practically family already." Ellen hoped the shaking of her head wasn't too vigorous. Keeping her gaze shifting around their surroundings, she hoped her smile was merely pleasant as she could feel Constance's sharp gaze examining her profile.

"All the better, I'd say. None of this awkwardness that would come from wedding a veritable stranger. And even if Richmond thinks he'd rather put it off, now that he's the only one left, he does not have the luxury of doing so, unless he wants to see his family's estate fall into the hands of some long distant cousin or perhaps revert to the Crown. It could be considered that you'd be doing him a favour by setting your cap at him."

Ellen laughed again despite her continued discomfort. "I'm not certain he would see it that way, but I do see what you are saying. But never mind Hugh, who else should we consider?"

"Hugh, is it?" Lady Constance asked pointedly while arching her perfect eyebrows at Ellen, but then she laughed and turned the subject slightly. "Well, I did see you dancing with him last night, so it cannot be so very uncomfortable for you to consider him, can it?"

Ellen shrugged coolly, though her cheeks warmed in a contradictory fashion. "As I said, there are many reasons to consider other options. You are the one who was set upon this topic, you must have some other ideas."

"Well, there are any number of eligible gentlemen, really. Perhaps we ought to start with considering what you think you would like to see in your mate? Are you determined to find a handsome gentleman?" With those words, Constance wiggled her fingers in a wave at one who was passing by, and Ellen prayed fervently he hadn't heard her. "Or wealthy? Or powerful? Do you want a husband who has no mother so you needn't worry about a mother in law? What do you wish for?"

Ellen shrugged. She had really just met this woman. She wasn't sure she was ready to divulge all her innermost thoughts to her. She forced a light laugh.

"It seems to me this conversation has veered into far too complicated corners. Why don't you tell me about where you are from? And your family – do you have sisters or brothers who have accompanied you to Town?"

With that Lady Constance went off on a rambling description of her family and their home. It didn't require a great deal of Ellen's attention to follow along with what she was saying, so she allowed her gaze to wander about.

With a start, she recognized Lord Richmond and Mr. Northcott across the park. They appeared to be deep in conversation. While she was watching, they were approached by another man, who appeared far less *tonnish* than they were. Her curiosity was piqued, but they were too far away for her to do anything except observe. She also, for reasons she couldn't explain even to herself, didn't want Lady Constance to notice the men's exchange, so she tried to subtly change the direction of their journey. Or perhaps she could explain it. Constance was a talker, a busybody. And she had already pointed out Hugh in far too uncomfortable a manner just that morning. She certainly didn't want her to return to the topic.

But what was Hugh doing speaking with Gilbert Northcott? How was it possible that two of the men on her list were speaking that very morning? Of course, it was entirely possible that they knew each other in the small world that was the *ton*. But she was highly uncomfortable nonetheless.

"And that is how we ended up with both a commoner and a foreign prince within the family."

Ellen blinked. She had not been paying the least bit of attention at the end, as her attention had been so firmly ensnared by what Hugh and his acquaintances might be up to. Heat flushed through her, and she hoped she didn't cause hurt feelings to her new friend.

She smiled weakly. "You must miss them," she finally thought to say, thinking that might be a safe, neutral expression.

The other lady shook her head. "As I mentioned, we aren't particularly close, so I'd rather receive periodic, exciting letters from them than to have to share a house with them. And I will admit that I am relieved that I haven't had to share my Season with either of them."

Ellen laughed, relieved that this time it was neither forced nor fake. "I was thinking the same thing, that I don't want to share my Season. I thought that made me dreadful. I'm relieved to know I'm not the only one." She paused then, in thought. "I must say, though, there might be certain advantages to sharing. I was nervous as we descended those stairs into the ballroom with what felt like all eyes trained upon me. If I was there with my sisters, it could be reasoned that the attention was divided."

"But do you really want the attention divided? Can you imagine how absolutely dreadful it would be if your sister was considered more popular than you? My sisters are beautiful. I'm sure they garnered immense amounts of attention. I would have felt quite overshadowed, I can assure you."

Ellen wrinkled her nose. It was hard for her to think of her sisters in this light. But the other woman probably wasn't wrong. It would have been completely different with either of her sisters in attendance. Some parts would have been lovely, and others might have been dreadful. She shrugged. It mattered little. Theodora was already married, and Amelia was still considered too young. And if Ellen had her way, she too would be well ensconced in a new life before her younger sister made her own curtsey to Society.

"Very well, then, how about Viscount Adelaide?"

Ellen started at the sudden turn of the topic. "I haven't yet met him, but he strikes me as being a rather indolent fellow. I'm not sure if he'd be a good match for me. And eventually being Countess of Everleigh sounds dreadfully responsible."

"Well, he's highly eligible," Lady Constance countered with laughter in her tone. "You are proving quite firmly that you need to give some thought to what you're wishing for in your husband."

Ellen was still unprepared to discuss the matter, so she turned it on her new friend.

"What are you looking for, then?"

"Well, as you know, I have no intention of wedding this Season. But when I do start to consider it, I will expect my husband to be wealthy, titled, handsome, popular, and influential."

Ellen burst into laughter, thinking Lady Constance was surely exaggerating, but when she only stared at Ellen in question, she brought her laughter under control and sobered quickly.

"That is quite an extensive list of requirements. Perhaps you ought to consider Lord Adelaide for yourself."

"Perhaps I will. It seems to me he isn't on the Marriage Mart, despite his attendance at most Society entertainments. It is possible that when I am ready, he might be as well."

"I think a quieter existence might be more to my taste," Ellen excused and then hoped to turn the subject. "Are you promised to the theatre this week?"

"Have you a box?" Lady Constance demanded.

Ellen smiled. "It was my mother's indulgence for the Season. She said it was the thing she enjoyed the most when my sister Theodora had her Season, and her only regret was that they had to await invitations from others. Mama was determined that this year she could be on the side of extending the invitations, rather than awaiting the receipt. And now she can go whenever she wishes."

"That sounds lovely. Your mother at least is bright enough to learn from her experiences."

"You should join us sometime. I don't think we actually have anyone planned to join us when we go this week. If you'd like to join us, I'm sure it would be fine."

"You had best check with your mother first," Lady Constance countered but seemed delighted by the invitation.

Ellen was burning to turn and check on Hugh and his associates but still wasn't comfortable allowing her companion to notice. Finally, they were hailed by some other young women they had met the night before, and the chatter quickly overtook any discomfort Ellen had been feeling.

Chapter Four

"You want me to do what?" Gilbert sounded incredulous. Yet he remained in step with Hugh along the Park's path. "I don't even properly know what the Home Office does. How could you possibly think I could take over some sort of mission on a moment's notice? Surely, there must be some sort of training to do something like this."

"I will tell you everything you need to know. And you are right to be cautious, as it will be dangerous. But I cannot complete my mission myself, and I will not be able to live with myself if I do not ensure it is carried out. It is a matter of security for all in our great nation." Hugh kept his voice low and his body relaxed in a regular stroll despite the vehemence in his tone.

Gilbert stared at him as though he had lost his mind. "Doing it a trifle too brown there, aren't you, old fellow?"

"I'm not, actually." Hugh's smile was pleasant, belying the seriousness of his words. No matter how important the matter was, he wouldn't want a casual observer to take note.

"So you're telling me that you're a spy? And none of us ever suspected?"

Hugh gestured with a finger to his lips to remind his friend to keep his voice low.

"Spy is such a negative word. I seek information for the benefit and protection of our king and country."

"So a spy," Gilbert repeated with a dry chuckle. "It sounds far more exciting than I ever thought you capable of."

"That is actually the point," Hugh pointed out.

"What made you think I could take over your precious mission?"

"I've known you since we were boys. There's no one I trust more than you and your brother and a few of his friends."

Gilbert's face hardened at that. "You would have asked Adelaide if you could." He'd stated it rather than asked, and Hugh cringed at the evidence of the old rivalry between brothers.

"Considering my situation, you have to know why I couldn't ask Adelaide. In fact, for that very reason, I wouldn't even ask you if I weren't desperate."

"Thank you very much," Gilbert replied with sarcasm dripping from his tone.

"Desperate for someone I know I can trust and who I know can actually accomplish what needs to be done."

"But how do you know I can do it?" Gilbert wasn't being falsely modest. Like any gentleman, he considered subterfuge to be beneath him. It was a challenge for a man of gentle birth to stoop to such a level. But their loyalty to the Crown usually won them over.

"Why did you never enlist?" Hugh turned the subject slightly.

Gilbert stared at him with a frown. "The earl wouldn't hear of it."

"Exactly. But you wanted to, didn't you?"

Gilbert shrugged and nodded.

"Why?"

"Duty, I suppose. And an expectation that I ought to be caring for others."

"This will fulfill that feeling," Hugh explained. "Listen, Gilbert, if you find being an agent isn't to your taste, you can decline any future assignments. But I need someone to do this for me. And I cannot entrust it to just anyone. I can't even allow the Office to reassign it. I cannot explain it to you properly. But I will feel as though I've let everyone, including myself, down if I do not ensure this is carried out properly. And there are very few I would trust to grant me that feeling. I will beg if you make me."

Gilbert suddenly grinned. "While a part of me would dearly like to see that, I shan't make you. Very well, you have convinced me. But do say we'll keep this between us for the time being at least. It wouldn't do for the earl to find out. And I quite like the idea of having something over on Adelaide as well."

Hugh wasn't about to argue with the other man's reasoning. He didn't rightly care what reasoning Gilbert needed in order to accomplish what Hugh needed him to do.

Their long acquaintance assured Hugh that once Gilbert agreed, he would follow through and accomplish what Hugh needed from him. It was one of the many reasons why he had been so determined to speak with the man. He knew he could count on Gilbert, and that was what he needed most at that moment.

It probably hadn't been the wisest move to arrange this meeting with Gilbert Northcott at the fashionable hour. At the time, Hugh had figured since they were both gentlemen of Society it wouldn't be out of the ordinary for them to be seen together in the Park. But Hugh couldn't be relaxed and unconcerned about this subject, and he was afraid his intensity might be noticeable despite his best efforts. He quickly glanced around.

His assignments at the Home Office had honed his skill for being always aware of his surroundings. He had a tendency to be a trifle lax about that ability when he was somewhere he considered "home" or when he was too wrapped up in a matter. It took concerted effort to remain constantly alert. Hugh suddenly regretted having relaxed a little in the other man's company. He realised he was allowing himself to become too comfortable as Viscount Richmond. He needed to remain Mr. Turner, the competent, well reputed spy a little longer.

Assessing his surroundings let him know that it was far more crowded than he had expected. Hugh suspected that more time might have passed than he had been aware of. He had thought they had time to discuss their matters and it would appear as any natural encounter. But just as he was about to dismiss his concerns, they were approached by an unsavoury looking character.

Gilbert stiffened at his side, but Hugh was pleased to see that he stood his ground. It boded well for his ability to take over Hugh's mission. Despite being high *ton*, the man was clearly able to be tolerant of others.

"I've been searching for you, m'lord," the rough man greeted, appearing furtive. Hugh grinned despite his irritation that Shawn would approach them so publicly. Shawn was one of his best couriers, most able to blend into the least savoury of environments, less capable of fitting into a Society location.

"What are you doing here, Shawn? You know you ought to meet me in the mews, not here for all to see."

"But things have become urgent, m'lord. Seems to me you ought to be doing something about it, not dallying around with your fancy friends."

Gilbert laughed, to Hugh's relief.

"Is this the sort of thing I am to expect then, Richmond?"

Hugh nodded at his friend and watched as the other man stepped forward and introduced himself.

"It would probably be best if we were to acquaint ourselves with one another elsewhere. But I am Gilbert Northcott. I have plenty to learn. And you can probably help me with that."

Relief flooded through Hugh at his friend's acceptance of the situation in front of him. He had already been certain Gil Northcott was a good choice for the assignment, but it was reassuring to see that he hadn't been wrong. It was a relief to Hugh that despite his distractions, his good judgment of character was standing in good stead. In fact, it was somewhat surprising that the Home Office hadn't seen Northcott's potential and approached him themselves previous to this. Not that it mattered. He had agreed, and he was now in a position to solve Hugh's main dilemma. Now Hugh could carry on with the business of being Viscount of Richmond.

Not that he actually desired the role.

But what else was there for him to do? He couldn't repudiate his inheritance. This was not how he had foreseen his life turning out, but most would envy him. He knew he was being ridiculous to lament the turn of events.

Besides the immense grief he felt at losing both his brother and father in one fell swoop, though, he was also grieving the loss of the life he had loved. The life of an agent for the Home Office had perfectly suited him. And now he would have to learn to take his Seat in Parliament and all that would entail. He was again relieved that he had at least been taught plenty about the estate as a boy so it wouldn't be the worst thing ever. It just wasn't what he had wanted.

His watchful gaze noted that the passing gentry was eyeing him and his strange choice of companions. One lady in particular, Hugh could tell, was trying to hide her interest, but there was avid curiosity glowing in the gaze that kept darting back and forth between her destination and him.

It was Lady Ellen. She was far too intelligent for his good. He would have to take his leave of the others as soon as possible to mitigate any damage.

Chapter Five

Just as she was almost to her own front door, Ellen frowned as she turned her head at hearing her name hailed from the bottom of the stairs. She had just walked home from leaving Lady Constance at her front entry. Her maid had left her to run an errand, explaining they were in desperate need of new ribbon. Ellen had allowed herself to become consumed by her thoughts once she was finally alone and was therefore unprepared to hear from Hugh. Almost as though her thoughts had conjured the man. It was most disconcerting.

"Good afternoon!"

Lord Richmond seemed far more jovial than she had ever seen him in recent years.

"Good afternoon, my lord. I am surprised to see you so quickly."

"So quickly?"

Ellen's frown deepened. He appeared to have no idea what she was talking about.

"Yes, I just saw you in the Park. I wouldn't have thought to see you at all, but certainly not this soon as I just saw you."

"Did you, now?" Richmond returned her frown. "Do you have a moment that we might talk in private?"

"That is hardly seemly, my lord, but you'd best come into the house. It won't do for us to be bandying words here on the front stoop."

He bounded up the stairs toward her, agile and light upon his feet. Ellen was momentarily distracted by his attractive presence. But she was even more shocked by his seeming desperation to speak with her.

Suddenly, the one thing she had been putting from her mind since she had found out he would be in Town could no longer be pushed aside or forgotten. She had tried to forget. Oh how she had tried. But now, for no explicable reason, all Ellen could think of in that moment was *the kiss*. The only kiss she had ever experienced. And it was from the very skilled lips of the handsome man currently towering over her. Uncharacteristic anger swept through her.

"What do you want, Richmond?" She didn't care how rude she sounded. She wasn't going to tolerate his nonsense. She was in Town to find her match, and she would hopefully be able to leave again quite quickly. She needn't see Hugh, Viscount of Richmond, any more than absolutely necessary. Ellen questioned her sanity for a brief moment. What had she been thinking when she had actually put Hugh on her list of potential mates? It was obvious he was not for her. She was relieved she had already crossed him off.

"Could we speak privately, El? It's important."

"That's Lady Eleanor to you, my lord, and as I already told you, it's a dreadful idea for us to seek private speech."

"You hate being called Eleanor, so I'm not about to start that. And I swear I shan't compromise you. You can fetch a servant, and we can leave the door open, but it's most urgent that I speak with you without all and sundry being privy to the topic of our discussion."

"You swear you shan't compromise me, do you? I don't see how I can believe that," she tossed back at him even as she preceded him into the cheery front receiving room that was just off the entranceway they were currently arguing in. Ellen wasn't even certain how they had gotten there from the stairs, as she had no recollection of the necessary steps.

The expression on Hugh's face indicated to Ellen when she turned to face him that he too was suddenly thinking about that kiss almost four years ago. She had only been fifteen years old when she had given the handsome young man her heart. He had barely turned twenty. She should have known they were too young to wed, but her heart hadn't been the least bit interested in listening to any sort of logic. Besides, they had servants who wed at that age. Ellen hadn't seen why it would be so very impossible for them.

They had been at Hanley House, in the home generations of Courtenays had been raised in. Hugh was visiting Ellen's brother Jeffrey as a lark before he departed for his Grand Tour. He had seemed far more grown up and serious than on previous visits. Ellen had fallen desperately in love and had been certain the feelings had been reciprocated.

Most of the fortnight Hugh had spent with Ellen's family had been entirely involved with Jeffrey, but he had taken the time to speak, dance, and play any manner of games with the three Courtenay girls as well. They all thought he was the most wonderful creature ever to have graced their halls. But only Ellen had truly fallen in love with him. Or so she had thought. Of course, she assured herself frequently, it couldn't have been true love. She was far too young for one thing. For another, surely true love would have to be reciprocated to truly be, well, true.

But humiliation still burned through her whenever she allowed herself to think about the aghast expression upon Hugh's face when the very perfect moment in his arms drew to a conclusion.

"My deepest and most sincere apologies, Ellen, but I cannot marry you."

"I don't recall having asked you, Hugh. I would have expected you to do the asking, for one thing." She hadn't thought through her answer, it had just tumbled out of her when he had made his ridiculous statement about not marrying her.

"I'm leaving next week for my Tour."

"I know that."

"And I've just kissed you far more thoroughly than a gentleman ought."

Ellen had grinned. "I know that, too."

"But I cannot marry you," he had said it firmly, despite the evident anguish on his face. Ellen couldn't begin to guess why he would be so torn up on the subject.

"I can wait for you to return," she had said, but his suddenly implacable expression had made her hesitate and it had come out as a question rather than a determined statement.

"I cannot marry you, Ellen. I should never have kissed you. I am so sorry. I cannot offer you any sort of promises. And I cannot explain myself. Promise you will forget me."

Ellen had stared at him in confusion before anger had saved her. "I find that an easy promise to make. I've forgotten you already, Hugh." She had swept from the room and never seen him again until she had encountered him the night before at her first ball.

Apparently she had done as she had promised. She hadn't prepared herself for encountering him. Ellen had completely forgotten her humiliation and anger in recent times despite the agonies she had gone through for years after his departure. It was the most foolish thing yet about this Season. How could she have possibly forgotten? And yet she hadn't forgotten, not truly. She had merely shoved all the thoughts and feelings aside and chosen to ignore them. They no longer wished to be ignored.

Turning her mental back on the unwelcome memories, Ellen faced Hugh and didn't care that she would appear confrontational and belligerent.

"What do you want Hugh? Don't make me ask you again. I'd like to keep this conversation as brief as possible."

"I thought we were friends, Ellen," Hugh countered, sounding a trifle desperate as he ran his hand through his curls, causing them to appear rumpled in a dashing sort of way rather than disreputable. Ellen despaired. Why would he be even more handsome now?

"I don't know why you would think that."

"You seemed pleasant toward me last night when you asked after Jeffrey."

"I was desperate for information," she reminded him. "Is that why you've come? Do you know something I ought to be informed about? I had actually thought it might take another day to learn anything."

"No, my courier hasn't returned yet, probably I will know by this afternoon." He paced away from her suddenly. "So you were only being pleasant because you wanted something from me? Is that what you're telling me?"

Ellen shrugged. "Not exactly. I had kept my promise of forgetting all about you, to be honest, Hugh. But when I saw you last night, I remembered your long friendship with my brother and asked if you knew anything. It was you who promised to send a courier. I didn't think of that." She was relieved that her voice sounded quite reasonable now. What a conundrum. How could she get him to leave? What could he possibly want with her? Suspicion started to mount within her chest as she remembered her momentary thought when she'd seen him in the Park.

"Yes, yes, of course. I seem to always be apologizing to you, but once again I must do so. I'm sorry, Ellen. I haven't been myself just lately."

Ellen wanted to go to him and offer the comfort he so clearly needed. But she hardened her heart instead.

"I must ask why you were speaking with Mr. Northcott this morning, Richmond. You did not want me for yourself, but surely you cannot think to interfere with other possible matches for me, can you? What could you possibly benefit from ruining my future any more than you already have?"

Ellen watched while all colour drained from the handsome face before her.

"Have you been promised to Northcott?" he demanded. "He said nothing of it to me. I swear to you, Ellen, we were speaking of another matter that had nothing to do with you."

Ellen's always too tender heart felt as though it were bleeding from the drama it was experiencing that morning.

"Then once more, I must ask what you want, Hugh. If it is not in connection with your conversation with Mr. Northcott, then I do not see why you had to hustle directly from there to here. Surely you must see why I came to that conclusion."

Hugh again raked his hand through his hair and sighed.

"It *is* in connection with Northcott in a certain way, but I didn't think the two of you were already connected."

Ellen frowned in confusion but shook her head. "We aren't connected. I just don't wish to dally here in Town any longer than necessary, so I am considering all the possibilities. We danced last night, and he was pleasant."

"So you consider that the only criterion for husband? Surely you must set a higher standard for yourself, Ellen."

"I do not see how it is any of your concern, Richmond." She put gentle emphasis on his title in an effort to remind both of them that there was only formality between them now, despite their closeness years ago. "Please, do get to your point. You requested privacy or secrecy or what have you. You shan't have it much longer if Mother hears of your presence, surely you realize."

To her surprise, the strong, serious man before her blushed like a youth, and he was suddenly awkward and stumbling.

"You are correct, El. I must get to my point." Ellen refused to be softened by his use of the diminutive form of her name even though she had always loved to hear it in his deep voice. The passage of time had only improved upon it.

But he appeared far too nervous to act upon his words of getting to his point. Finally, Ellen's glare loosened and she had to laugh. She had to forgive their youthful selves. Hugh had apologized at the time of the offence. She supposed it was herself she needed to forgive. Especially for the feelings she had secretly and foolishly held in trust for the handsome man standing before her suddenly so indecisive for the first time since she met him. With a shake of her head, Ellen knew she wasn't yet ready to forgive either of them. But she could relent at least a little. She forced her fists to unclench and took a deep breath in order to release some of the anger she knew had been in her tone earlier.

"Tell me, Hugh. I'm sure it must be important or serious for you to have approached me like this. I shouldn't have allowed old anger to fester and spew onto you. That part was my fault, not yours, and is why I was suddenly suspicious of your association with Mr. Northcott." She looked around as though seeing her surroundings for the first time then gestured behind him. "Won't you have a seat and tell me what brings you by?"

He sat but still appeared dumbstruck so Ellen smiled and gently prodded again.

"If you're not here to speak of Jeffrey nor Mr. Northcott, have you suddenly recalled that you promised to tell me all about your Grand Tour and your conscience would not allow another moment to go by?" She grinned at her foolish suggestion. "No, it cannot be that or you would recall that my mother would want to be present for such a conversation. I cannot actually even begin to fathom a guess. Shall I ring for tea service while you gather your thoughts?"

Suddenly Hugh was laughing, and he once more looked like the handsome youth she remembered from her idyllic childhood. Ellen felt a little more of her anger dissipate even as a part of her wondered why their youthful selves hadn't been able to make a match. But it mattered very little now, she persisted in thought, she was going to make a perfectly acceptable match as soon as she could figure out what Hugh wanted from her and sent him on his way.

Chapter Six

"Ellen, you are a delight, whether you are angry or conciliatory, you are always unique. I have missed you and your family quite desperately and hadn't even realized it."

Once the words were out of his mouth, Hugh realized they could be considered somewhat insulting, but to his relief the girl laughed. He supposed she was no longer such a girl. She had grown up to be the beautiful young woman he had known she would be on that last, ill-fated visit, just before he took up his first assignment for the Home Office.

Visiting the Courtenay family at Hanley Hall had been his own private little good-bye festival to his old, pre-agent life. He had accidentally given his heart to the sprite before him those years ago. Hugh had never wished for it back. He had always thought he would continue a solitary existence as an agent for the Crown. There had been no room in his life for a wife or for feelings of any sort except for his loyalty to his assignment and the patriotic impulses that he cultivated to maintain that loyalty. But now everything was different.

Except not completely. Until Northcott was able to take up the assignment and get the information Hugh had been so close to getting when his mission had been interrupted by news from home, Hugh wouldn't actually be fully free. For his own peace of mind and for the safety of their nation, Hugh needed Ellen's cooperation.

"I need you to swear your secrecy, Ellen," he began earnestly, watching as the laughter drained from her face. "And while you're swearing, I need you to swear your fealty to King George."

The intelligent gaze of his long-ago love never wavered from his face as she searched it for some hidden meaning. "Why would you need me to swear to those things? Surely, having known me since I was a little girl, you should know that loyalty to our King and country are facts of my life. And I have never betrayed a secret. And well you know it from your own experience." Ellen crossed her arms in a defensive gesture.

Hugh would have blushed if not for the fact that he had been a hardened agent for several years now. But the woman's words caused him a level of discomfort he never would have expected. Clearly, she was harbouring a grudge against him. And he couldn't blame her in all actuality. He had betrayed her trust by kissing her and then leaving. He ought to have offered for her immediately despite how young she had been at the time. As she had said, she could have waited for him.

He sputtered a reply. "Yes, of course, you were always such a reliable friend."

But he had never expected to inherit. What prospects had he had as a younger son? It had been necessary for him to make his own way in the world. He had been quite successful in doing so as an agent. Even if he hadn't inherited, he would have been in a financial position to make an offer to any young woman. But as an agent, what kind of life would he have really been able to offer her? Visitations a couple times a year? While that might have been acceptable to some, it wasn't the type of life he would like to establish for his own family. Remaining alone, unwed, had always seemed like the wisest course.

Except now he had inherited and his life as an agent was coming to a close.

Would Ellen consider his suit now? The thought tantalized him much like a mirage he had once seen when he had become too thirsty while travelling in a hot country. He was still not in a position to make an offer for any woman, not until he had well and truly turned over his life as an agent.

The sooner he got this all behind him the better. Now that he had accepted that his life was turning in a direction he had never expected, he wanted to get on with it as soon as possible.

Giving his head a shake, Hugh realized Ellen was still gazing at him expectantly and looking a little puzzled. He was dithering. After his dramatic demands for her promises, he hadn't followed through with what he needed from her. He shook his head again and sighed.

"Perhaps you are right; we ought to sit down. And I need to hurry up, as you pointed out. If I wish to keep things confidential, it won't do to tarry."

He followed his words with action and stepped toward the seats she had indicated, gratified to hear by the rustle of her skirts that she was following his lead and taking a seat as well.

"Spit it out, Hugh. You are being mysterious and odd all at once. Do tell me what is going on and how I can be of assistance."

He couldn't restrain his grin despite how serious the subject was. Ellen was always impatient for information. It was part of the reason why he knew he would have to speak to her after he saw that she had noticed him in the Park. He wished he could just tell her a half truth and keep her out of this business, but he was sure she would be able to sense any prevarication on his part.

"When you saw me speaking with Gilbert Northcott, it had nothing to do with you," he began, surprised when her watchful gaze barely changed expression. He supposed she hadn't truly believed that he was that underhanded to attempt to sabotage a potential relationship for her. He carried on his explanation.

"I have been working for the Home Office for just over four years now."

This statement finally caused a change in the woman's expression as her brows drew together and her chin dropped down in surprise. But she still didn't say anything. She continued watching him carefully, as though not wanting to interrupt and trying to understand what he was saying to her.

"My first big mission or investigation was the last time I saw you. Or rather when I left Hanley Hall, I went straight into it."

Her face softened at this, but she still said nothing, so Hugh continued.

"Some would consider it underhanded what I do. But I have become convinced that knowledge is power for our country. And that power and knowledge can prevent wars and therefore save countless lives. So I don't care what anyone thinks. I know I have been doing my duty."

Now her head tilted and a frown formed on her brow. “Why would anyone think less of you for seeking knowledge?”

“I would be considered a spy,” he stated baldly, but her expression didn’t change. In fact, she shrugged.

“I suppose it all depends on the perspective with which you look at the situation,” she finally said with a grin. “Whoever you are spying upon might not appreciate it, but if, as you say, war can be averted, everyone should seek this outcome, I would think. But isn’t it dreadfully dangerous, Hugh?”

Hugh’s heart felt as though it had rolled over in his chest. He hadn’t truly felt anyone had cared about the outcome to his own person in years. And to have this slip of a girl, the same one he had actually wronged so long ago, express this first concern made him wish he wasn’t too much of a gentleman to pull her into his arms and kiss her senseless once more.

Heat swept through him. Was this why he had come to speak to her? Because he hoped to regain his place in her life? He had risked his mission as well as her safety just because he allowed his feelings to get involved? What a ridiculous notion. He would have to think about this at another time. Now was certainly not the time nor the place. He had to finish this matter first.

Being the experienced agent that he was, he managed to get his mind straightened out in the blink of an eye. Perhaps a long blink, but he managed it. He would castigate himself for the fool he was later.

Finally he mustered a shrug.

“Yes, there has been some danger involved. But that matters little now. Unfortunately, my responsibilities to Richmond now require that I leave the service. So the worst danger I shall be facing in the future is whether or not I ought to fence in the bull separately or together with the herd."

This produced the chuckle he had hoped for from the watchful woman before him.

"But why did you make me swear, Hugh? What are you not telling me? And what prompted you to tell me this little bit now?"

"Ah yes," Hugh said with a grin, appreciating the young woman's quick mind. "I saw you in the Park. It was evident you were trying to hide your watchfulness, but I know that you saw me there."

His eyebrows rose as colour stained her cheeks.

"I did see you, and I didn't want the lady I was with to notice. I cannot even tell you why; it felt instinctive. But are you about to tell me that there was a reason why I didn't want Lady Constance to notice you? A reason that makes more sense than just a feeling I had?"

Hugh grinned, a sense of well-being washing over him for the first time in years, perhaps since the last time he'd seen her. He didn't want to feel that way about her, as he wasn't in a position to be able to do anything about that at the moment. But he would accept and enjoy the sense of well-being for as long as it might last. He knew enough about life to realize that such a sensation ought to be cherished as long as it was available.

"Yes, I am trying to finalize my last assignment for the Home Office. I feel duty bound to ensure it is properly cared for. I cannot fulfill it myself, of course, now that I have become Richmond."

"I'm sorry, Hugh." Her softly uttered words of comfort went straight to his midsection. Fluttering began around his heart, and his stomach turned over in an almost pleasant way. He shoved those feelings away. A sense of well-being was welcome. Anything warmer was not.

He cleared his throat and carried on. “Yes, well, of course, inheriting was a surprise, and I now have to change everything. But I cannot allow my last assignment to go unfulfilled. I also cannot allow you to involve yourself in it.”

Ellen frowned. “I hadn’t realized I had done so,” she said in a slightly frosty tone.

“You were watching us so attentively, Ellen. Do recall that I’ve known you since you were still wearing your hair down and your skirts weren’t so long.”

“You might have known me as a child, Hugh, but you chose to cut off all association for the past four years. I am no longer that little girl who could not contain her curiosity.” She made as though to rise to her feet but then quelled the impulse. Hugh smiled. She had always loved to pace when she was upset or thinking through a matter. “I was curious. That was all. I wasn’t about to interfere with any matters of national importance, I can assure you. I am in Town to participate in the Marriage Mart. It is as simple and as complicated as that. There was nothing for you to be concerned about, I can assure you quite absolutely.”

There was a brief moment of silence between them that felt quite fraught, but then Ellen lightened it with a smile.

“Now, having said that, I can no longer stick with that statement. You have come here and explained how serious and important your assignment is. Now I do want to be involved. I hadn’t intended to involve myself, but you have now made it impossible for me to ignore what has taken place.”

Hugh stared at her and then groaned. He could never admit his own foolishness to the lovely young woman before him. He still needed to gain her forgiveness. How likely was she to offer it if she knew he was a simpleton? "For a man experienced in subterfuge, I didn't do this very well, did I?"

Ellen laughed. "So, tell me what to do to help."

"Nothing, Ellen, I swear it to you. I need you to stay safely out of the way so I can get this matter cleared up."

"I don't believe you, Hugh. You wouldn't have come here just from the fact that you saw me across the glen at the Park. Why would you do that? You must have wanted to involve me whether you want to admit it or not."

"Ellen, you cannot be involved. It is far too dangerous."

Ellen stared at him. A glance toward the floor revealed to Hugh that one of her feet had begun to tap. He supposed she was irritated with him. She twitched as though she wanted to cross her arms but again controlled the impulse. Hugh was impressed with the level of her self-control. She hadn't been like that as a girl.

"I suppose I could just ask Mr. Northcott about the matter," she finally said with a musing tone.

Hugh could see one of her dimples fluttering to life in her cheek. He remembered that she had always hated the crevices that appeared in her cheeks, but he had always enjoyed them. They made themselves evident when she was amused, even, it would seem, when she was trying to hide her amusement.

"You cannot allow Northcott to know how much a fool I've been to approach you like this."

"How have you been a fool, Hugh? You might not wish to admit it, but you know I could be of great assistance in any matter. I was always the very best at hide and seek or any games of strategy when we were children."

"I would readily admit that. But I do not want you involved, as it is quite possibly going to be dangerous. Swear to me that you shan't approach him on this."

"Are you going to accost me if you see me talking to him at the next ball?"

"I don't attend balls, Ellen, I'm still in mourning."

"I just saw you at one last night," Ellen protested with a frown.

"I was there for a very specific reason," he insisted firmly

"And yet, you took the time to dance with me. Or was that your very specific reason?"

Again a fraught silence settled between them as they stared somewhat belligerently at one another. Finally, Hugh allowed a low chuckle to escape him.

"Please, Ellen, I'm begging you, swear to me that you won't involve yourself in this. I will not be able to concentrate as I must if I have to fear for your safety."

"You have to know I cannot swear to that. You should have thought of these concerns before coming here. You are the one who has involved me, Hugh. I did not stick my nose in your affairs."

Hugh stared at her. She was right. He was a dolt. He should have realized there was no way she was going to be able to ignore this now that he had involved her so thoroughly. And he had involved her. Not the other way around, no matter what he might wish to think.

"Ellen, please, you mustn't. I know, it was foolish of me to come to you like this. And perhaps, in the unconscious recesses of my mind I wanted your involvement, but truly, logically, and most assuredly, it is not safe for you to be involved."

She stared at him hard for a moment, making Hugh squirm a little. Then, in a very soft voice, she proceeded to destroy his sanity. "But is it safe for you, Hugh? Who shall watch over you just as you wish to protect me?"

He wanted to scoff at her but managed to restrain himself. "Are you thinking to offer your services in protecting me, then, little one?"

At that, she sat up straighter in her seat. "I will." She said it so simply as though she needn't give the matter any thought. Such loyalty despite what he had done to her was thoroughly undeserved. A shudder ran through him.

"I deeply appreciate your wish to assist me, but I cannot accept, I'm afraid." He even put up his hands as though to ward her off.

"Hugh, let me put it to you like this: you can allow me to assist in some way that you will know about, or you will have to worry about me courting scandal by following you about and making a nuisance of myself in order to ensure your safety. Or I can send for my brother to come see to you, if that might make you feel better. It would be far less satisfying for me, but it might make more sense. Really, Jeffrey ought to be here anyway. But that just brings us back to the conversation we had last night and whether or not your courier has any information for us." She sighed and laughed lightly. "So really, it seems to me that you just have to accept my help whether you want to or not. It really is quite inevitable."

After staring at her for a moment with his mouth agape, Hugh finally nodded and accepted the truth of her words. There was really no choice in the matter.

"I will take you for a drive tomorrow. We will discuss it then."

With barely another word, he took his leave of her.

Chapter Seven

Ellen was left blinking in the breeze that he left in his wake. Metaphorically, of course, she thought with a dry chuckle as she shook her head over his abrupt departure. She wasn't quite sure what to make of their visit that afternoon. She didn't really want to think about it though, as that way lay trouble for her heart. She had already wept all the tears she intended to cry over that particular man.

Ellen walked toward the window that looked out over the busy street. Just in time to see Hugh urging his team of horses out into the traffic. She shook her head. The poor man had clearly not been thinking. If he wanted to keep his visit a secret, he probably shouldn't have left his curricle out for all to see. He was clearly growing used to being Viscount of Richmond rather than Hugh the secretive spy.

It wasn't something she would complain about, though. Even if he had no interest in her, the suspicion that he might was likely to create a bit of gossip that could lead to other gentlemen being interested in her. She would accept the unintended gift. Hugh owed it to her after their shared past.

But still she couldn't dismiss from her mind that she was concerned about him. In many ways, really.

The poor man had lost his much loved father and brother only recently, as well as the unexpected new responsibilities that have now landed upon him along with his sudden loss. And as it turned out, he now had to give up a position she hadn't known he had but that he seemed to really cherish.

Why would any gentleman wish to trade in espionage?

She hadn't really reacted to it when he had first told her, but now the very thought gave Ellen a shiver of fear. But she would override that fear if it meant helping him stay safe. Even if he was an experienced agent, Ellen knew men didn't always look at things in the most logical order. Take the events of that very afternoon. What had he been thinking to confront her like that if he actually didn't want her to know that he was an agent? If he was making blunders like this, he clearly needed someone to look out for him. Perhaps his grief had turned his mind somehow.

She couldn't, though, stand by and allow him to be in danger. Ellen wondered if she ought to send for her brother. Really, Jeffrey ought to be in Town seeing to her debut anyway, along with Father. If Jeffrey were there, she wouldn't have to give Hugh the least thought. In her brother's absence, she couldn't help but think she ought to do something.

Not to say she would have the first idea of how to watch over a grown man like Hugh. But she was willing to learn. It was only for the sake of their long ago friendship, she tried to assure herself, but Ellen was afraid it might be more than that. The flutter in her midsection led her to believe that the feelings she had thought long dead might be trying to experience a resurrection. That could not be allowed to be true. No matter what, Ellen was determined to find the comfortable match she hoped for and to retire to her new country estate at the first possible opportunity. Helping Hugh would have to be just a minor little distraction. It could not be allowed to interfere with her own plans for her comfortable future.

That all being said, though, she couldn't leave the man to his own devices.

With a decisive nod of her head, Ellen turned her back on the view to the street and headed to her bedchamber, calling for her maid as she went. She had some strategizing to do before that evening's entertainments.

Some hours later, Ellen had the sensation as though she had donned a suit of armour when she examined her reflection while her maid put the finishing touches to her hair after her gown had been eased over her head. She wasn't certain if it was the thrill of feeling involved in something important or just the excitement of having visited with Hugh again, but Ellen was in her looks that evening. Mother would be thrilled. She had been lamenting Ellen's pallor the night before, claiming that gentlemen wouldn't be interested in her if she appeared sickly. Examining her reflection more closely, though, made Ellen wonder if she might still appear sickly if her colour was too high and hectic.

Margery, her maid, interrupted her critical thoughts as Ellen was waving her hands in front of her face to cool off her heated cheeks.

"You are looking even lovelier than I've ever seen you, my lady. You will be sure to turn heads tonight."

"Thank you, that's so kind of you to say. I was worried I might look feverish."

Margery laughed. "You are the most unnatural worrier, my lady. You don't look the least bit feverish. Now get on with having the best time and be sure to remember all the details to tell me while I brush out your hair tonight."

Ellen grinned at the maid who'd been a part of her life since she was a child. The young woman had been trained to be her lady's maid after having cared for her so well when Ellen was a wee girl. Sometimes it felt to Ellen that the maid was more her sister or aunt or even mother than her actual family members, as she was always so actively involved in her life. And the servant was often far more encouraging than Ellen's own mother with never a critical word on her tongue.

"I'll have plenty to tell you tonight as I already have things I haven't told you yet, but I think I need a little bit more information before I unburden myself."

"Oh no, my lady, that's right unfair of you to say. Now I'll be wondering all night."

Ellen laughed and jumped up from her vanity table to pull Margery into a quick hug before hurrying toward the door. "I'll tell you everything tonight, I swear it to you."

With those words and her maid's laughter spurring her on, Ellen hurried from the room to join her mother on the drive to the famed Chorley ball. Theodora had met her husband at the Chorley Ball during her debut, and Ellen had always hoped that she would as well. Her excitement knew very few bounds. She just knew she was going to have an exciting night.

When they arrived at the ball, Ellen cringed once more at how she was announced, but she forced herself to ignore the reaction. It really mattered very little, she assured herself. Anyone who became a true friend would be able to soon learn her preferred way of being addressed.

She tried to be discreet as she looked around the room searching for Hugh. She shouldn't be searching for the man, as she knew he was not the one for her, besides the fact that he had assured her he was not in Society due to his mourning, but it couldn't be helped. She had given him her heart and even if they couldn't wed, she knew she had to ensure he was safe.

A part of her hated that he had become an agent. It seemed so underhanded. Hugh had always struck her as someone who was honest in all things. But that was foolish to think, considering how things had ended the last time they'd seen each other. Anyhow, whatever the case, she couldn't allow him to do it on his own.

If she could help, she would do everything in her power to do so. As he had asked her, was she loyal to the Crown? Of course she was. So if his investigation was of that sort of importance, who was she to turn her nose up at it?

Since Hugh wasn't yet present, Ellen needed to get her focus back on the original matter at hand – the husband hunt. Tonight was supposed to be the night in which she found her match, she reminded herself as she tried to focus on the very important matter. She had her list of requirements always at the ready in her mind. She needed to weigh it against each gentleman she was introduced to.

Take Lord Adwell, for example, she thought as he bowed over her hand and swept her into the minuet that was just forming, carefully avoiding a spill of wax that had accumulated on the floor. It was good of him to ensure her safety. That was surely a note in his favour. She smiled at him in appreciation.

"Did you come up to Town well in advance of the Season or have you just arrived?"

Her puzzlement over his question must have been written across her features as he was quick to elaborate.

"When my sister made her debut, she and Mother came weeks in advance to arrange for Sarah's wardrobe. Mother insisted that nowhere in the region of Adwell would have the quality materials they required."

Ellen almost bit her lip to prevent its quiver of amusement but managed to swallow both the impulse and her laughter. It would seem Lord Adwell fit most of her criterion for a potential husband as he was clearly of good family and had sufficient wealth to keep her in a lifestyle she had grown up with. She didn't need to marry someone with the very deepest pockets, but since she had always lived in comfortable circumstances, Ellen had no desire to learn how to pinch her pennies. Family was another important factor to her, but her family tree wasn't terribly extensive. She would hate to not expand it through marriage.

With a nod, she acknowledged his words. "The shops near Hanley are sufficiently well stocked that we didn't have to come to Town early. Perhaps it is because we are situated closer to London than Adwell."

His frown indicated he didn't appreciate her observation. She tried not to return his expression. While kind and pleasant were already items she considered important on her list of husband requirements, she wondered if she ought to add a lack of arrogance. She couldn't really expect a gentleman to be humble, but he needn't consider himself the most important creature to have walked the earth.

She turned the subject, hoping to see if he could match her other two requirements – well read, and possessing all his teeth. He had yet to smile, so she couldn't be sure. Ellen wasn't going to be so shallow as to require he be exceedingly handsome. Appearances can fade over time. But she did expect her husband to be known for being kind. Again, she had her future children to think about. And while she didn't want to refine overmuch on appearance, she would set the bar low and require that he have all his teeth. She really didn't think she could bear to sit across the breakfast table from someone who was missing his.

"Have you found any circulating libraries in Town to suit you?" she thought to inquire, adding a broad smile at the end in the hopes that it would be returned. Instead the man's expression barely changed, and her heart sank.

While she expected to marry a man who probably enjoyed many things she would consider dull such as sport or hunting, she also expected to be able to carry on enjoyable conversations with him about literature or plays or some such. And if he could teach her something he had learned, she would consider that a bonus.

Ellen had thought her list was broad and vague enough to allow for a wide range of eligible gentlemen, but she was disappointed to note that many of the men she had so far been introduced to were not what she would deem pleasant. She started to wonder if she was just too provincial in her sentiments. Perhaps haughty didn't necessarily translate into unpleasant. But she could not see herself being comfortable with a man who thought he was that much her superior. She stifled a sigh as she curtsied to Lord Adwell after he he brought her back to her mother's side. She was certain she had not yet met her future husband.

It didn't help her concentration on the Husband Hunt project when she finally saw that Hugh had arrived, despite his insistence earlier that day that he wouldn't be in attendance. Of course, his entrance was far less spectacular than that of a debutante, but Ellen still noticed it somehow. It seemed to her as though they were attuned to one another when their eyes met across the crowded ballroom. Hugh was the first to avert his gaze. And he didn't once approach her during the brief period that he was present.

Since she was performing the steps of a *contredance* at that moment, Ellen was forced to mind her steps rather than the way her heart rate had kicked up upon seeing the handsome viscount. It seemed he was determined to ignore her despite how their gazes had clung. He hadn't even nodded in greeting.

Ellen told herself he wasn't hurting her feelings, but she didn't quite believe it. Perhaps he wasn't deliberately hurting her feelings, but it hurt nonetheless. After the rather intense conversation they'd had that afternoon, she had rather expected that their relationship had turned a corner of sorts and they could return to the friendship they had enjoyed as children. At the very least, she would have expected that he would approach to greet her.

It would seem that had been a foolish supposition on her part. She only hoped the gentlemen in the current dance didn't notice how damp her palms had grown.

Chapter Eight

Hugh had to force his gaze away from Ellen's when his eyes met hers across the crowded ballroom. She was a vision in the creamy coloured gown that seemed to float around her. He had never seen a more beautiful woman. But he couldn't be thinking such thoughts. He had a war to avert, if at all possible.

He turned his mind forcibly away from the fact that Ellen was searching for a husband and concentrated on the matters at hand. In point of fact, he had barely noticed that Gilbert had approached him.

"How's your Spanish?" Hugh asked the other gentleman, who only stared at him in dismay.

"Dismal at the moment. I cannot say that I've ever spoken a word of it. But my French is excellent, as was my Latin when I was in school. From what I understand they are closely related, so I might be able to pick up quite a bit."

Hugh nodded. "You should understand a great deal, but you won't be able to express yourself very well in a short time. I had suspected as much. You will need a companion to accompany you. I know just the fellow. It is why I attended this evening."

After the introductions were performed and it seemed as though the two gentlemen would be able to get on well together, Hugh made good his escape. He needn't be present at such a large social event, in fact, he ought not be. He could plead his state of being in mourning.

"*Disculpe.*" Hugh heard the Spanish word, and his feet nearly froze in the action of walking away from the Chorley Ball. He managed to not betray himself, though. It was a challenge even though it shouldn't have been. He was getting slack in his home country. He was used to always being on guard. His instincts took over, and his steps didn't even falter.

"*Perdón, señor.*" This time the voice was louder and closer. Hugh's ears were attuned to the accent and emphasis, and he knew he was being addressed by someone from the region of Spain where he had been skulking most recently. "Excuse me, sir. I suppose I ought to use English, since I'm on English soil." This statement was followed by an epithet Hugh couldn't quite translate, but it was evident the speaker wasn't happy about being in England. Reluctantly he paused in his attempt to leave the area and turned toward the woman speaking to him.

"Are you speaking to me?" He asked it as innocently as he could muster, hoping the surprise on his face was only that of being addressed in a foreign tongue and not shock over the speaker's appearance. Because the woman before him was an exotic beauty.

His eyebrows twitched. Could she possibly be a spy when she was that attractive? He surmised that it would be a challenge for her to hide or avoid detection. But then again, the best spies were a lot like chameleons. He had often felt like one himself. And he suspected that someone trying to get close to him would think they needed to be highly attractive to get his attention. Little did she know, he preferred the simple country beauty of an English debutante rather than an exotic entertainer like her.

"*Sí, señor.* I would speak to you a moment, *por favor.*"

Hugh knew there was trouble on his horizon, but there was nothing for it but to see what she wanted. It was a good thing that he was already leaving his assignment with the Home Office if his identity had been compromised.

"We have been following you, Hugh, Viscount of Richmond." The woman stepped toward him, her voice dropping to a near whisper. "We know that you used to be Mr. Harrison and also Mr. Turner and that you have been spying on us. We have known this for a long time." She paused, probably for dramatic effect, but all it did was make Hugh feel sick in his stomach. "You have been especially active since San Ildefenso, *tengo razón.*" Again she paused, and it took all Hugh's considerable experience to keep a pleasantly puzzled expression on his features. "And we know how seriously you have taken your work. So, some in our circles expect that since your foolish English sentiments will require you to retire from actively pursuing us, you will find someone to replace you."

Hugh swallowed down his instinctive reaction. He supposed he shouldn't be so shocked. The spy trade required a keen understanding of people. And he didn't think he would be so terribly hard to read. He *had* thought his identity had been better covered, but that was probably overconfidence on his part. But now everyone he had spoken to while in Town was at risk of exposure.

"The problem is, you have met with so many that we cannot be sure," she was continuing with what she no doubt thought was a seductive purr, but all it did was stop the blood in Hugh's veins. "Except the woman."

Hugh's heart froze in his chest before it began beating at triple its usual rate and felt as though it were trying to jump right out of his chest.

"It is obvious she means something to you. We thought your aristocratic ideals would prevent you from recruiting a woman, especially one of noble birth, but we could be wrong."

"I have no idea what you are on about," Hugh suddenly remembered that he ought to be dissembling. 'Admit nothing' had been drilled into him from the very beginning of his training as an agent.

"Yes, you do," she replied with arrogance.

"If you think I am a spy, why are you telling me this?"

"You have been a worthy adversary. There is honour amongst us, at least a little."

Hugh stared at her for a couple beats of his frantically pounding heart. "As you said, I am a viscount. My only involvement in anything to do with Spain is as pertains to a trade agreement that was discussed in Parliament a few days ago."

"For such an experienced spy, you do not lie very well," she purred with a taunting smile. "I will bid you goodnight."

Hugh could hardly stop her. It was the most uncomfortable interlude of his life. He stared after her and wondered what he ought to do first. He needed to warn everyone, but where to start? And then it struck him. They were counting on him to panic. Despite their claim of having watched him and knowing him well, they obviously didn't know him at all. He would never have been so successful within the Home Office if he was one to give in to panic. A smile touched his lips. He had the perfect solution.

~~~~

Ellen had received him in the same room in which they had spoken when he had told her about his assignment. This time, she wasn't bothering to sit still as she had tried to do the first time. "I beg your pardon." Her tone didn't sound the least bit like it was begging, but Hugh found her outrage delightful. Ellen was never boring. For now, though, he couldn't allow himself to become distracted. It sounded to him as though he had offended her.

"I need you to become betrothed with me." He repeated the words as succinctly as he could.

"For your mission," she added in a stunned tone. "The one that you are reluctant to leave off," she tacked on. "You do realize that marriage is a life-long assignment, do you not, Lord Richmond?"

She said the last bit so sweetly, if he didn't know her so well, he might not have known she was dripping with sarcasm.

"We wouldn't have to go through with it," he assured her.

"Why would I agree to such a preposterous arrangement? You do realize I am in Town for the Marriage Mart, do you not? It will ruin my prospects if I were to become betrothed at this point. And then to terminate the betrothal very well could ruin me completely. And it's not just me. If I become known as a jilt, what is to become of Amelia when she makes her debut?"

"In two years? Ellen, surely, Society will have forgotten all about this little episode."
~~~~

"It's possible that they'll forget *why* I'm on the shelf, but the actual fact of my *being* on the shelf will make things more difficult for my sister." She paced away from him, but he could still see the outrage on her face or at least quivering through her arms as they waved in agitation at her side.

"Ellen, you will not remain unwed. You are beautiful, intelligent, and well dowered. This will only disrupt your life for a few weeks, I promise you."

She whirled back toward him with an arched eyebrow.

"I'm not beautiful," she scoffed. "Not like that wonderful creature you were speaking to as you left the ball last night."

Hugh's eyebrows lifted toward his hairline. "Are you absolutely certain you don't work for the Home Office? If you don't, you ought to."

She surprised him by laughing. "Perhaps I *will* take up the service. Especially if I am to remain a maiden for the rest of my days."

Every sensation within Hugh revolted at the thought of her remaining unwed. But he also rejected the thought of her wedding anyone else. He was being a dolt.

"It's for your own safety, Ellen, and perhaps even that of your family," he finally admitted.

She stared at him, and he suffered through the sensation that she was reading his every thought.

"In what way would our betrothal keep me and my family safe?" She was frowning and sounded suspicious, as though she thought he might use such an excuse to get her to agree. He might, if necessary, but in this case it was true.

"That woman you saw me with last night? She knew about my work. And she was following me. Or perhaps she had others following me. But she has noted our association and thinks you are to be the next spy."

Ellen laughed in disbelief. "Me? But I'm the most boring creature in existence."

"Hardly," Hugh drawled. "And it really isn't that farfetched. You would be brilliant at it, as I already pointed out. Except for being a noblewoman who has never had to do for herself," he added with a grin. "But in any case, if we become betrothed, they will no longer suspect you of being my replacement. They will realize that our involvement with one another was courtship, not spy craft."

Ellen stared at him for far longer than was necessary, making Hugh squirm a little.

"This will be very challenging for my mother. I cannot decide if it's best to keep her uninformed or not."

"We cannot tell her about the mission. Look what has come of me involving you. It is better for her and us that she not know the truth of the matter."

Ellen's nose wrinkled in a most attractive way. Hugh was almost distracted by the errant thought. *How could a nose wrinkling be attractive?* Surely he was losing his mind.

"She will be most disappointed in me when we end our association," Ellen explained with a sigh. "And how awkward will it be for your friendship with Jeffrey?" She sighed again and gazed at him morosely. "Are you certain this is our only option?"

"It's not the only one, but I am certain that it is the best one."

"Explain to me what you get out of this. I understand you think I am now in danger because this

Spanish woman thinks I might be your replacement as a spy. So our betrothal will explain away our association as being of the romantic sort, not the spyish sort. And this will keep them from trying to eliminate me, I suppose. I can see your logic. But what good does it do for you?"

Hugh frowned. "I would never be able to live with myself if something were to happen to you as a result of your association with me. None of this was your fault. I wasn't thinking clearly and jumped to a conclusion, and now here we are. Something that has never in all my days happened to me, I might point out. So I must ensure you are protected."

Ellen nodded but continued to look at him expectantly.

"I need this mission to succeed, Ellen." Hugh could hear the slight desperation in his voice, but he didn't try to cover it up. He needed to convince her. "It is my last one. I need it to not be a failure. Or *I* will feel like a failure."

Ellen's ever empathetic inclinations quickly jumped to the fore and she made as though to come toward him with comfort to offer, but Hugh held up his hand to prevent her approach. He should have known she would turn soft.

"Don't misplace your sympathy on me. It won't fail. But I cannot worry about your safety and the mission's success all at once. I need you to be safe. And the men will look after themselves."

"Have you warned them?"

He nodded. She nibbled her thumb as she paced about the receiving room a little bit more. Finally she sighed and nodded.

"We cannot allow it to go on overlong, though, Hugh. I truly do not want to remain in the Marriage Mart for too long. And we'll have to come up with a good reason why we have decided we would not suit. Something people will believe but that shan't compromise me."

"Of course."

She sighed again. "Very well, then, I suppose you have a betrothed." She didn't sound the least bit happy about the prospect but then, in almost the blink of an eye, her face brightened and she laughed. "Would you take me to Vauxhall? It is considered far too racy for a debutante, but now that I have a fiancé to accompany me, surely it wouldn't be beyond the pale."

Hugh laughed. "You are going to be the death of me, aren't you?"

Chapter Nine

Ellen waited anxiously in her bedroom, not wanting anyone else to witness her fidgets and pacing. Hugh was speaking with her father about their betrothal. It made her feel ill in her stomach. How could they deceive her family in this way? It seemed the most underhanded of starts. And how was she to keep her heart out of the business?

To her surprise, her father and brother had arrived in Town on the heels of the courier Hugh had sent to ensure all was well at Hanley. As it turned out, there really had been a problem with the flock, but it had quickly been dealt with. Lord Hanley had grumbled quite heartily about missing the opening of Parliament, but Ellen was nearly certain the government had managed without him. Ellen wasn't certain how Jeffrey would react to Hugh's proposing to his sister, though. She only hoped it wouldn't damage their friendship when Ellen's betrothal came to an end. She chewed on her thumb in her distress as she paced the room in order to contain it.

They had agreed, when they had worked out this ridiculous scheme, to wait until today for Hugh to speak with Ellen's parents. First, they had put on quite a spectacle at the ball Ellen had been promised to that night.

Not that they went beyond the bounds of acceptable behaviour. They had only danced two times together. But one of them was the super dance. So they had spent a great deal of the evening in each other's company. This way, Hugh had explained, it would come as no surprise to anyone when they announced their betrothal. And even Ellen's parents shouldn't be surprised by his appearance seeking an audience that afternoon.

But still Ellen paced. And nibbled on her thumb. And straightened out all the little items on her dressing table before flinging herself onto her bed with a muffled screech.

How was she to get through the coming weeks? That was the worst part of the entire mess. Hugh couldn't tell her conclusively how long it would take to ensure their safety. He needed to ensure all the gentlemen he had spoken to were safe without telling them anything about his assignment. That in itself would be a feat of some accomplishment. Ellen's admiration for him would know no bounds if he managed to pull that off without stirring up a great deal of gossip.

And when had she developed admiration for Viscount Richmond, she demanded of herself as she climbed back off her bed and resumed her pacing. Considering he had broken her youthful heart, she was only doing this to keep her family safe, she reminded herself with a flounce even as she listened attentively for anyone sending for her. Surely he wouldn't leave without speaking to her. That would certainly belie their sham betrothal.

Suddenly, without her noticing the approach of feet, there was a scratch at her door, and Margery stuck her head into the room.

"Oh, my lady, there's excitement afoot." She nearly did a dance of joy as she sidled into the room. "A viscountess – how thrilling."

"Oh, Margery, don't get too excited just yet. I haven't told you everything I promised to. Are you here to collect me?"

"Not just yet. I'm sure one of the footmen will be along in good time. I just heard the whispers through the house and had to come see to you. Knowing you as I do, I thought you've probably messed with your hair or spilled something on your gown in all your agitation."

Ellen had to laugh over this. Her dear maid wasn't wrong. She glanced down her person. "I think I've managed not to make too much of a mess of myself, but perhaps you could tidy my hair."

"Sit yourself down and tell me what's troubling you."

Ellen quickly obeyed, anxious to unburden herself.

"You have to keep this confidence, though Margery, promise me."

Looking offended, Margery scoffed. "When have I broken your confidence?"

"Never that I know of, but it's just that important, Margery. Besides, the entire household loves to gossip."

"That they do, but you know I can tell the difference between what's to be said and what isn't."

"I know, I'm just so consumed by it all."

"Tell me quick and you'll feel better." The servant assured her even as she was readjusting the pins in Ellen's hair and brushing out pieces here and there.

Ellen sighed. "It's not real. Hugh is only becoming betrothed to me because of some mission he has been doing for the King."

Margery's chin dropped down in a satisfying display of shock. "Oh my lady, here I was thinking he had remembered his youthful love for you after all this time."

Ellen smiled through the tears that suddenly gathered at the words. "Nothing so romantic but nearly as dramatic."

"And you agreed to this?" Margery demanded. "I take it from the need for secrecy he isn't telling your parents his true intentions?"

"I did agree. As I said, it's for the King."

Margery's hum of disapproval was all that was needed to indicate her feelings. Suddenly, though, the footman was at the door and there was a tumult of activity while Ellen was bundled into her spencer. Within moments she was seated beside Hugh and they were bowling along toward the Park with her mother's congratulations ringing in their ears.

Silence had fallen between them. Finally, Ellen broke it.

"Was it dreadful?" her voice felt small.

"Deceiving two of my favorite people?" he asked for clarification. "I'm sorry to admit I've had a great deal of practice in the past four years."

Ellen nodded. "I know you're disappointed to be ending that life, but surely that is one thing to be happy about. You shan't have to play a role any longer."

"You don't think being Viscount of Richmond is a role?"

"Perhaps it feels that way right now, but it's at least real. You might not like that reality, but it isn't a lie."

It was only because she was watching him so closely that she noticed him clench his fist and then as though through the power of his will he forced everything to relax. It wouldn't have been terribly evident to a casual observer, but Ellen was far from that. In the blink of an eye, he was just as sunny dispositioned as usual.

"You were probably a terribly good agent weren't you?"

Hugh chuckled. "I'm surprised you would think so with the blunders I've made in the last se'en-night, including getting you involved."

Ellen nodded. "That was unfortunate; I have to agree with you. But some of the issue was me, let's face it. If I hadn't been so nosy or curious, it might have been a completely different story." Ellen shook her head even though he probably couldn't see her, as his attention was directed to driving his pair of horses. "I wasn't referring to that though. It's your uncanny ability to hide your feelings. That must have stood you in good stead in your work."

They lapsed into silence but it was the companionable sort. Having spent a great deal of time with him in the last two days, Ellen had grown more relaxed in Hugh's company. She was trying not to harbour her anger towards him, as it would do them no good in their current situation. And they had both been very young. Thinking about it would do her no good, either, so she thought conversation would be in order.

"Tell me what you have planned for Richmond." She had obviously surprised him as he turned wide eyes upon her.

"What do you mean? Do you think I ought to be making changes? I feel as though that would be presumptuous on my part, since I wasn't even supposed to inherit."

Ellen sighed softly and laid her hand on his arm. "But you did inherit, Hugh. You didn't go searching for it, you are certainly not responsible for their deaths, but it did happen, and now Richmond is yours. You cannot just leave it as is. And if you make some plans you can be enthusiastic about, surely that will help you accept the role that has been thrust upon you."

Hugh's intent stare at his horses' ears made Ellen think he was either ignoring her or deep in thought. Suddenly he turned that piercing stare upon her while still skillfully guiding his team.

"How did you become so wise?"

She shrugged and smiled despite the heat climbing into her cheeks. "That's what happens when years go by."

They again turned their gazes away from one another but conversation continued. Ellen couldn't have said if it was comfortable or not. She herself was full of conflicted feelings, but she was glad to be talking rather than worrying too much.

"I hadn't really given thought to making changes at Richmond, but now that you've given me the idea, I'm certain there are plenty of modernizations I could undertake. It would surely lead to it being more profitable, which will benefit the tenants as well as me and the estate itself."

Ellen nodded, pleased to see him growing in enthusiasm for the topic. "What do you do at Richmond? Is it mines or flocks or some other thing that I cannot think of at the moment?"

Hugh's rich chuckle caused an unwelcome flutter in her midsection. She had to ensure she didn't allow her feelings to grow out of bounds. Ignoring the sensation was a challenge, but she valiantly tried.

"Yes to all of it. I'm still learning. Even though I was always the spare, I was determined to do something else with my life, so I didn't pay a great deal of attention to the estate as a boy, and then I've been gone for years.

But for certain there are mines. Iron is the main thing we're digging out of the ground. But we're also increasing our cotton production."

"Cotton? That's so interesting. I thought it only came from India."

"Not at all. More and more is coming out of the Midlands. And from the reports I've been reading, it would seem my tenants are getting better at processing it as well. I can see that it will be a good thing for me to continue to learn more about. Apparently our steward had been trying to convince Father to try the velvet market, but he was resistant. I will take your advice and see about that."

Ellen warmed at the thought. She cherished the thought of giving him good advice. Or rather, she hoped it turned out to have been good. One more thing for her to worry about. She didn't like how this affair was turning her into someone who frets. She hoped it didn't have to drag out for too long. Her mind was going to turn into a shambles if she wasn't careful.

The rest of the afternoon passed in an enjoyable blur and before Ellen knew it Margery was helping her into her favorite ball gown and putting the finishing touches on her hair.

"If I didn't know any better, my lady, I would think you were quite in love. I've never seen you look so well."

Ellen's throat tightened with fear that the maid might be right, but she tried to brazen it out. "It's just the excitement of it all," she insisted. Margery didn't look convinced but didn't argue with her on the topic.

It shouldn't have been such a surprise, but it turned out being a betrothed lady during the Season was a far different experience from being a debutante. Ellen quite enjoyed the change as there was far less pressure upon her to have a partner for every single dance. Of course, she reflected, it was going to be a challenge to give it up when the time came. But for the moment, she supposed, she would enjoy it as Hugh swept her into his arms and onto the dance floor.

~~~~

Tongues were wagging, Ellen was certain, but not in a malicious way. It was highly enjoyable to discuss all the latest *on dits* with Hugh when he came to call each afternoon, including the ones about themselves. Each day he faithfully visited her whether he could stay for a long visit or not. They talked about books, the theatre, music they enjoyed playing or listening to, and further discussed his growing plans for Richmond.

Jeffrey, who seemed delighted that his friend was about to become his brother in law, would often spend time with them as well. Ellen couldn't decide if she loved those times or loathed them. She hated deceiving her family. And while she greatly enjoyed discussing Hugh's plans for the future, a part of her was beginning to wish she would actually be a part of them.

But they had agreed that he wasn't ready to actually settle down with a wife, and she wasn't willing to wait until he was, on the off chance that he would pick her. Maybe they hadn't actually agreed on that, but they had each stated their stand on the matter.

So now it was just a matter of waiting for his Spanish situation to be resolved and then they would terminate their betrothal. Ellen still couldn't think of a reason that they would give. No one would really believe they wouldn't suit.

Despite Hugh's still being in mourning, everywhere they went they were looked upon with approval. Ellen was surprised. She shouldn't have been, though. As with everything, the rules were often eased
~~~~

considerably for men than for women. She tried not to be irritated. It certainly wasn't Hugh's fault. And he was being a most attentive fiancé.

Her smile was genuine when he brought her a drink at a rout or sat with her at a musicale. And she greatly enjoyed his witty companionship when he escorted her to the theatre. She had enjoyed herself so much that she couldn't even remember what they had seen.

Ellen bit her lip as she gazed into her reflection one morning. She was enjoying their association a great deal. It was far more entertaining to view Society as a committed woman rather than a single one. She had no desire to remain single any longer. But maybe for Hugh she could change her stance. If all he needed was time, what harm would it actually do to wait? Just because Theodora got married within weeks of her debut didn't mean she had to do so. It wasn't as though their family couldn't afford for her to dither about in Society. She would, of course, need to wed before Amelia was ready for her debut, but surely she needn't rush her own choices. Lady Constance would be glad for the company.

With a sigh and a shake of her head, Ellen brought herself to task. Despite how compatible she and Hugh had always seemed to be, and their one kiss long ago notwithstanding, Hugh had given no indication that he had any sort of preference for her. She couldn't put her life on hold in the hopes that he might come to see her as anything other than a friend.

Their betrothal would have to end.

And so it was that ten days after they'd become betrothed, Hugh was finally escorting her on the promised excursion to Vauxhall. With wide eyes, Ellen held tight his hand as they stepped off the boat. She hadn't expected it to be so big.

Hugh had explained to her that they could have arrived by way of Westminster Bridge but that arriving by water would be far more charming. She couldn't argue with him. She was charmed.

"I've booked us a supper box but we are plenty early. We can wander around and see the entertainments first if you'd like."

Ellen nodded at his offer and held tight to his arm while keeping an eye out for Margery, who had been sent along as their only chaperone that evening. It had been quite a shock to her when her parents had agreed to the outing. She would have expected they would require at least there to be a party to attend.

"You're nearly married," Mother had said, "I needn't be quite so strict with you, I don't suppose."

After wandering through the ruins and statues and admiring the cascade, Hugh finally settled Ellen and Margery into their box and gestured for a waiter to bring them their food.

"I must warn you, though," he explained, "the suppers here aren't famous for their satisfying quality."

Ellen waved away his concerns. "I'm far too excited to eat much anyway, so it is just as well that it shan't be a heavy meal."

True to Hugh's word, the ham was thin and the rest was scanty, but as Ellen watched the mingling crowds of nobles and commoners alike she couldn't say she even tasted her meal such was her excitement. It had already been a long day for Margery, though, and she was far less excited over the prospects. Even as Ellen and Hugh got lost in conversation, the poor maid was falling half asleep.

"You stay here and watch my reticule, Margery; we are just going to go for a short walk before we head for home."

"Are you certain, my lady? I ought to stay in your company."

"And have you fall asleep on your feet? That won't do. We shan't be long, I promise." Ellen knew she ought to keep her maid close, but she couldn't drag the poor dear any further even though she herself was desperately curious to see more of the gardens.

"Your maid was right," Hugh said even as he escorted her away. "We shouldn't leave her behind."

"Just for a few minutes, Hugh," Ellen cajoled. "There's still so much I haven't seen. And she's too tired to enjoy it."

They made their way down one of the walks, hearing music being played somewhere in the distance. Ellen started to question the wisdom of her choice to insist upon the adventure as the air seemed to grow more dangerous. But then they came across a small pavilion with musicians and dancers and she was once again swept up into delight. As the entertainment came to a close, she could sense Hugh's gaze fixed upon her, and she turned her face toward his with a grin.

His lips connected with hers in a sudden rush of heat and sensation. For a moment Ellen felt as though she were riding a heady wave of emotion before the reality of her situation insisted upon being felt. Wrenching herself out of the arms she couldn't even remember stepping into, Ellen fought the tears that wanted to spill in reaction to the tumult within her.

"How dare you? It's just like the last time. You will kiss me senseless and then leave me to pick up the pieces." She would have slapped him except that he grabbed her hands before she could.

"Ellen, my dear, I swear it to you. I never meant you an insult."

“It doesn’t matter, Hugh. Take me home. And I do beg of you to finish this business as quickly as you can.”

She spoke barely a word to him the rest of the night.

Chapter Ten

Hugh didn't see Ellen again for three days. But he didn't sit around moping. He had allowed himself to get far too comfortable with the life of doting betrothed and hadn't concluded the business he had come up to Town for in the first place. He couldn't face her while she was still in danger. It was good he was getting out of active duty. Hugh had very quickly gotten soft in the head.

In those three days much had been accomplished. The Home Office had been able to move around various agents and associates within the country and abroad in order to stir up enough activity that Gilbert and Shawn's actions hopefully went unnoticed.

Hugh had spent time with the two men and was relieved to see how well they got on despite their very different stations in life. He wasn't there to wave them off, just in case he was still under observation, but Gilbert Northcott left London early one morning with Shawn by his side as companion, translator, and assistant. It had been a grey day and Hugh had paced for hours vacillating between worrying about what he might have set his friend up for and jealousy that his old friend would be just beginning the adventures he could no longer enjoy. But the fact was that Viscount Richmond could not be an active spy. So he focused on his relief that he had been able to pass the assignment to someone he trusted so well.

Further relief was felt when word was received that various arrests had been made. Foreign agents on British soil were no longer running free. And the mysterious woman who had approached Hugh that fateful night had disappeared quite promptly back to wherever she had come from, or rather, they were reasonably confident she was no longer in England. Hugh had done his best to describe her to Gilbert in order for him to remain on alert.

"You're beginning to sound like a nursemaid, Hugh," Gilbert had complained just before taking his leave. "You trusted me enough to ask me to do this, now trust me to do it."

Hugh had laughed and slapped his old friend on the arm in lieu of expressing any other feelings. The matter was now closed.

But Hugh didn't want it to end. Not the matters with Ellen at the very least. So, he talked it over with Lord Chamberlain.

"I'm being the daftest man in all Creation, aren't I, my lord?"

"I don't see it that way, son," the older man countered in his steady, unperturbed way. "You've had quite a bit of turmoil in the past six months. You've quite earned the right to feeling a bit confused."

"But that's just it. I'm not confused. I have accepted that my life as a true agent is over, although I must say I appreciate your offer of allowing me to do a few little errands for you from time to time," he inserted with a nod and a grin. "But I find myself actually looking forward to returning to Richmond and settling in as Viscount."

"So what seems to be the trouble then, son?" Lord Chamberlain's brow furrowed, but his eyes twinkled, making Hugh think he just wanted to hear him admit to the truth.

"I don't want to do it without Lady Ellen."

"What's to say you have to?"

"The fact is that I don't think she'll forgive me."

"Have you asked her to? Because if you haven't, then I might have to agree with you about the daftness."

Hugh laughed as the older man had intended, but his heart wasn't really in it. He hadn't yet asked her. He had every intention of doing so even though he held little hope that she would actually grant her forgiveness. She believed he had played fast and loose with her feelings even though that had been the farthest thing from his intentions.

After shaking Lord Chamberlain's hand, Hugh walked away from Whitehall, perhaps for the last time, but there was a lightness to his step that hadn't been there for a long time. He tried not to allow his hopes to climb, but it seemed he couldn't help himself.

When he banged the knocker at Ellen's family's London townhouse, Hugh was surprised to feel such nerves fluttering in his midsection as he had never felt before. Not even on his most dangerous missions had he been quite this anxious for success. His smile felt a touch grim as a footman opened to him.

"I will see if Lady Ellen is receiving this afternoon, if you'll just wait in the receiving room, my lord."

Hugh strode toward the usual room where Ellen received him praying fervently that he wouldn't be kept waiting long.

"Do you have news?"

Hugh turned quickly toward the open doorway, sucking in a breath at the pretty picture his faux betrothed made. Colour was high in her cheeks as though she had hurried to meet him or she was furious. He hoped it was the former.

"I do, in fact." He strode toward her, hoping to grasp one of her hands, but she put them behind her back and stood stiffly staring at him. "Can we sit?" he finally asked.

"We have solved the matter. Everyone has been dispatched with suitable stories to explain their absences if they were to be noticed. And my mystery caller has apparently left the country. You are no longer in danger, and I am officially no longer an operative." He said the last on a lowered voice, still keeping his secrets even though he had left his much loved work behind.

"Are you terribly sad?" she asked with a slight choke, making Hugh realize that she sympathized with him despite her anger.

"Not as much as I would have expected, to be honest. I think our conversations about Richmond helped. I'm excited about the improvements I can make there, both for myself and my tenants. And I'm eager to learn about Parliament. Also—" He again glanced at the open door and lowered his voice. "The Home Office said they might be able to give me an assignment here and there that would not put me much at risk but still keep me sharp."

"Oh, that must give you mixed feelings," Ellen exclaimed, softening her stiff posture.

"You are certainly correct. But I appreciated them allowing me to not abandon my post completely," Hugh dismissed.

"It is not an abandonment of your post, and well you know it. Your circumstances changed. They must understand that."

"You are right, and it seems that they do."

Silence descended between them for a moment.

"So I suppose our betrothal is no longer required, then, in that case. What shall we say is the reason? I haven't been able to come up with a good explanation, especially for my family."

Hugh held his breath, surprised and relieved that she wasn't ready to tell her family she had a disgust for him.

"Would you be terribly opposed to remaining betrothed?" His voice was slightly shaken, and he fidgeted in his seat.

"For how long?" Ellen seemed puzzled. "I thought our ruse would end as soon as the Spanish situation was sorted."

"Until we meet at the altar?"

Silence fell between them once again, and Ellen did nothing but stare at him in shock.

"You would go through with the marriage? But what about your mourning?"

To her surprise, Hugh shrugged. "As it turns out, no one, not even my mother, was much put out by our betrothal. There's really no reason not to go through with it."

She stared at him a bit longer, making Hugh highly uncomfortable. He knew his declaration was lukewarm at best. He knew she had enjoyed his company until he had kissed her in the Gardens. She hadn't wanted to listen to his apologies at the time; he would have to try again.

"Ellen, my dear girl, please say you'll forgive me for my forward behavior of the past and accept my suit."

Again, silence fell between them as she stared at him. He was relieved to see she was not repulsed, merely shocked.

"I don't think it's a good idea." She sounded reluctant as she answered.

"Why not? I swear I'll be an excellent husband."

Now her stare turned speculative.

"What does that mean to you?" she asked softly.

Heat tinged his cheeks, but he didn't back down.

"I will do everything in my power to make sure you're happy."

"But what exactly will you do to ensure that?" she persisted.

"Haven't you been happy these past two weeks?"

"I was." She sounded reluctant, but Hugh congratulated himself that she hadn't yet run from the room.

"Well then we'll keep doing that."

"Why?"

"I beg your pardon."

"No you don't, you're just biding for time," she countered with a slight laugh. "Don't be a ninny. Tell me why you suddenly want to go through with our sham betrothal."

~~~~

Ellen's stomach was in knots. She had been furious when Hugh had kissed her at Vauxhall, certain he was going to kiss and run just as he had four years ago. It had dawned on her in that moment that she had fallen in love with him during the time they had spent
~~~~

together in their faux betrothal. Or perhaps she had never fallen out of love with him from when she was a young girl so long ago. But whatever the case, she couldn't wed him if it was merely an obligation on his part. She couldn't bear to be married to a man she loved who couldn't love her back.

He fidgeted a little bit more but to her shock, he suddenly threw himself onto the floor at her feet where she was seated in the least comfortable chair in the room. But she barely noticed her discomfort, so caught up in the moment was she.

"It's not a sham for me. I know when I demanded you become betrothed to me I said it was to keep you safe and to protect my investigation, but it was really just an excuse. I didn't fully realize it at the time. But I should have become engaged to you years ago, when we shared that first kiss. I never should have left you in such a shabby way."

"Why not?" she demanded.

"Because I love you quite madly, and I was a fool to think I could live without you. Returning to London and being in your company again has proven that to me. Do, I beg of you, Ellen, say you'll have me. I'll do everything I can to make you love me in return."

Ellen allowed a heartbeat to pass before she stood and pulled him up before her. Finally she shrugged.

"You really needn't do anything more. I've loved you since I was a girl. I'm likely to love you until the grave. I'll happily remain betrothed to you."

"But only until the altar," he countered with laughter that was quickly cut short as his head descended and he sealed her lips with his own.

Epilogue

Two years later

Ellen cradled her rounded belly as she leaned against her husband on the settee.

"I can't believe Amelia is having trouble with her debut," she said to Hugh as he perused the letter she had just handed him. "I'm glad Adelaide is giving her a little guidance, but it's odd that Jeffrey isn't there yet. If you'll recall, it was the same for my debut. He and Father were both absent when I first made my entrance into Society. At least she has Father."

"And just look where that led to for you," Hugh said, glancing up from the letter with a twinkle in his eye. "From this letter, though, it doesn't sound as though she's finding much comfort in your father's presence as he is far too busy with House business."

Ellen stared off into the middle distance causing Hugh to question her. "What are you thinking, my dear wife?"

"I'm remembering the trouble I got up to when the Season wasn't completely to my liking."

Hugh frowned. "As I recall, you were quite enjoying your Season. It was my interference that took it off its rails."

"In the very best way," Ellen agreed promptly, leaning in for a kiss from her beloved. Despite the pleasant distraction, though, she couldn't quite get her sister off her mind. "Do you think we ought to go up to Town and see to her?"

Hugh cast a significant glance at her midsection. "I suspect you wouldn't last long in a carriage before you'd be presenting me with a child," he said before grinning. "Or is that your intention?"

Ellen laughed. "I wouldn't be disappointed to have this little one in my arms rather than in my belly, I cannot argue with that. But I am a little worried about Amelia. It isn't like her to complain. Or rather, it might be like her to complain, but it's unusual for her to think she isn't excelling at something. And I feel as though Viscount Adelaide would be the least likely to assist her. It seems to me all he does is gossip and take snuff."

Hugh couldn't quite meet her gaze after that statement, and Ellen immediately noticed his reticence. "What is it that you know and aren't telling me, my lord?" she demanded with mock severity. "I have my ways of extracting information out of you."

"I know you do, my darling, but this isn't my secret to tell."

Ellen's eyes lit up. "So you admit that there is a secret." She threw herself into her husband's arms and proceeded to delightfully torture him into telling her everything.

The End

Keep reading for a sneak peek at the first full-length sweet regency romance novel which features Gilbert's brother Lucian, Viscount Adelaide, and Ellen's younger sister Amelia.

Intriguing Lord Adelaide is available in Kindle Unlimited, Kindle, paperback, and hard cover.

If you liked this book, please join Wendy's newsletter to stay up to date on all her fun news.

Join today at wendymayandrews.com

Sneak Peek!

Intriguing Lord Adelaide

BY WENDY MAY ANDREWS

~~~~

She's a wallflower debutante—and his best friend's sister.

But one dance could change everything.
~~~~

Chapter One

Lord Lucian Darius Northcott, Viscount Adelaide, was waiting for his father to die. It was the most lowering situation in which to find oneself. He didn't wish his father ill in the least. And yet, the entire purpose of Lucian's life was to replace his father as the Earl of Everleigh one day. In the meantime, he waited.

Of course, the extended purpose of Lucian's life was to produce an heir, who would then wait for *him* to die. It was a rather disheartening thought. And one for which he had very little enthusiasm, despite the fact that he dutifully participated in the Marriage Mart each year. He had important things to accomplish before he set up his nursery. Dangerous things. He couldn't very well do those with a wife in tow.

Despite his feelings, no one could rightly accuse the Viscount of Adelaide of shirking his duties. His utter boredom with said duties, on the other hand, was legendary. Even though he was a popular guest with Society hostesses, Lucian was always very careful not to allow any one young lady in particular to get the idea that he might actually be interested in wedding her. Until he was finally ready to accept his fate and become a married man, he at least had the sense not to allow anyone to entertain hopes that would go unfulfilled.

He knew enough about unfulfilled hopes that he had no desire to be responsible for them in someone else. But he also held out the faintest glimmer of hope that one day, he would meet a lady who would make him change his mind and take a chance on marriage, no matter his involvement with the Crown. That heir to await his death wouldn't produce himself.

While he had never felt love other than the filial variety, he had witnessed the fortunate happenstance of a couple of his friends' marriages that appeared to be truly happy and loving. It wasn't the norm, one might even say it rare, thus he had no idea where his hope sprang from, but he continued to hold out that tiny bit of hope that he might one day attain that blessed state for himself.

But waiting was becoming a dead bore.

With an inward roll of his eyes toward his own foolishness, Lucian pushed himself away from the wall he was leaning against indolently. He supposed he ought to do his duty toward the female guests and dance with some of them. With a quick glance around he ascertained that his earlier impressions were correct as to who was in attendance. He would easily be able to dance with both the Season's most popular debutante as well as one of its most persistent wallflowers. That should keep the tongues from wagging too specifically. And please his hostess.

He was going to ask Lady Charlotte, the Earl of Metcalf's daughter, to stand up with him for the next dance. She was that Season's most successful debutante and not a dreadful companion. Lucian had been surprised the first time he was introduced to her to find that she wasn't the simpering ninny he had expected her to be. But before he got near enough to speak with the girl, he was assaulted by the bundle of annoying energy that was his friend's little sister.

Lady Amelia Courtenay never failed to set his teeth on edge. Because of Lucian's friendship with her brother, Baron Hastings, he didn't feel he could give her a set down, but he was sorely tempted many times.

"Luce, you must save me," she declared with her usual flare for drama.

"Save you from what?" he scoffed. "I haven't noted a single ferocious beast present this evening."

"Well then you clearly haven't had your eyes open," Amelia replied drily. "I wouldn't have involved you, but it was simply unavoidable. Don't be a beast, Lucian. I need your help."

"What you needed was an extra year in the schoolroom. Then you might have learned that you shouldn't be addressing viscounts by their Christian names while you're about in Society."

"My lord, your eminence, please do me the utmost favour and dance the next waltz with me."

Now Lucian stared at her in consternation. While the young woman never failed to irritate him, there was always an unexpected current of *something* he experienced when he was unable to avoid dancing with her. He didn't want to deal with that something tonight. But how could he refuse what should be a simple enough favour?

Before he could come up with a suitable excuse, the orchestra struck up the opening notes of the next waltz. With Amelia looking at him with such a determined, expectant expression plastered on her face, there was nothing for him to do but offer her his elbow and escort her onto the dance floor.

One thing Lucian could say for Lady Amelia was that she was an excellent dancer. And when she kept her mouth closed, she was even a pleasant companion. But she inevitably ruined things by speaking or rolling her expressive eyes over something he said. It never ceased to annoy him. He rather thought the relationship would be similar if he'd had a sister. Though he supposed he'd spent enough time in her home with her older brother as a youth, Lady Amelia was very much like the little sister he never had. He stifled his sigh and started a conversation with her, despite knowing the risks.

"Tell me why dancing the waltz with you was such an urgent matter this evening, Button, and perhaps I'll consider helping you with the matter."

"Don't call me Button," she began, "and you've already helped me by dancing with me, so I don't really have to tell you."

Lucian stared at her with the haughty expression that had never failed him in the past. Or rather, it had never failed him with anyone except the chit in his arms.

"And don't bother trying to whither me with your noble glare, Luce. You know I've been immune to it since I was about twelve."

"Which was what, last year?"

Finally, the girl rolled her eyes even as she relaxed into the steps of the dance. For a moment, Lucian actually relaxed, too. Dancing with this annoying young lady never failed to put him into a sense of home. It was the strangest sensation. But he supposed it was because he had done it so often when she was a child. And her home had always felt more like a real home than his, despite the love he had for the noble old pile that was Everleigh.

Allowing his mind to drift, Lucian wondered why it was that Hanley House, Lord Hanley's comfortable estate, was more home-like to him than his own. He suspected it was because there were no expectations of him at the Courtenay home, other than to be a well-loved guest, which was how Jeffrey's family had always made him feel. On the other hand, at Everleigh, the expectations of him were unending and heavy. Which was why he had spent so many of his school vacations as far away as he could.

His father had never stood comfortably for that, of course, and had insisted that he come home at least some times. So, while Lucian did have particularly complicated feelings toward his birthright, he loved it nonetheless and felt a great deal of respect for the role he would one day take on. In the meantime, though, while it was still in his father's possession, he made sure to spend ample time elsewhere.

"Lady Fanny was making fun of me for being a wallflower."

Lucian was almost startled from his contemplation by his companion's words. She had become so quiet, he had nearly forgotten she was there, which was most unlike her. When the meaning of her words sank in, he had to swallow the profanities that immediately rose to his mind to keep himself from expressing them.

"I beg your pardon," he finally managed to say. Even he could hear the hauteur in his tone but fortunately, the girl realized it wasn't necessarily directed at her and she managed to muster a grin.

"Which part are you questioning, Luce?"

"First of all, Button, you really ought to be calling me lord while we are in company. For another, why would that dragon have the nerve to make fun of you? And why would she be so ridiculous as to call you a wallflower?"

"She might be a dragon, but she isn't wrong." Now Lucian was surprised to note that the girl would no longer meet his gaze.

His eyebrows rose. While he prided himself on his keen skills of observation, he had to admit that he had avoided keeping too close an eye on this particular lady. He had no interest in examining why that might be. But since she had made her debut, he had spent very little time with her. Now that he was finally looking, he noted multiple changes in her, obvious even in just their short time together. Lucian wondered if the girl he knew had matured into a different sort of woman or if there was something else going on.

"What do you mean?" he asked with a frown. "You couldn't possibly be a wallflower."

"Why not, Luce?" she demanded with an answering frown of her own before she corrected herself. "Apologies — my lord," she added at the end with a slight grin.

"I wouldn't think your brother would stand for it, for one thing, nor your sisters. For another, you're quite lovely and surely have a decent dowry. I would have thought you'd be extremely popular."

Lucian watched a variety of emotions that he couldn't quite pinpoint move across her expressive face. She was obviously gratified that he thought her lovely but took exception to the rest of his words.

"What is Jeffrey supposed to do about it?"

"Threaten anyone who makes you feel like a wallflower, for one thing."

He was gratified to see genuine amusement finally trickle into her expression.

"I'm certain that would surely make me very popular," Amelia countered sarcastically while continuing to follow his lead perfectly. Lucian could see that they were drawing the admiring gazes of many of their fellow guests. "While I don't really think threatening anyone would be in keeping with Jeffrey's inclinations, he hasn't come to Town for the Season yet. And for various reasons, mostly involving increasing their own families, my sisters haven't been able to join us, either. They have each repeatedly written flowery messages of best wishes and instructions, but I'm not finding it much help beyond the abstract. I appreciate their thoughtful words, but they haven't actually been of assistance."

She never missed a single step of their dance but looking into her expressive eyes, Lucian realized that her distress was very real, even more so than her light banter was letting on. He tightened his grip on her for a moment, wishing he could offer greater comfort.

"Have I not danced with you enough, Button? It seems to draw attention."

"Don't call me Button, *Luce*," Amelia returned, placing determined emphasis on the name he had admonished her for using. "And no, you haven't danced with me since my come out."

"Really? I thought for certain that I had."

"Well, you haven't," she insisted. "Apparently, I would find it more memorable than you would. Not that it would necessarily make that much difference," she added with a sigh. "The fact is, I just haven't taken."

"Why not?"

Amelia's grin did strange things to his equilibrium, leaving Lucian to wonder if he had drunk too much of the watered-down punch.

"I appreciate the fact that you're probably trying to make me feel better, but retelling the facts isn't going to do that."

"But how can I help if I don't understand?"

"Why would you bother?" Her question wasn't belligerent; she seemed as though she genuinely didn't know.

"You're one of my people." The statement made sense to Lucian but not to his companion, if her furrowed brow indicated anything.

"I'm reasonably certain we aren't related, Lucian, despite the fact that you spent half your childhood at my house."

"I didn't say we're related, my lady, I said you're one of my people. Did Jeffrey never tell you about our people, our kin?"

"He did not."

Lucian sighed. How was he to explain the tight bond he and his friends felt? His brothers were included in that kinship, of course, but sometimes, some of his friends, like her brother, felt more like his brothers than his siblings did. "It started when we were very young, our first year in school together. We banded together and made our own little family to stand up to the older boys. I'll tell you more about it some other time. Right now, you need to tell me how you could possibly be unpopular during the Season. Even if you don't feel like telling me. I promise, it will make you feel better."

"Just because you will it, my lord, doesn't make it so," Amelia countered in a quiet voice, barely discernible over the orchestra and the constant hum of the conversations whirling amongst the assembled guests.

"Just get it over with. I shan't allow you out of my sight until I've had a full explanation."

Amelia gusted another sigh, but this one sounded more resigned than irritated. "I don't think there's enough time left in the waltz to explain it all, Lucian, my lord."

"Then I'll take you driving tomorrow. You can tell me then."

"I don't think you should, my lord. It wouldn't be kind to my mother."

Lucian prided himself on his superior understanding. He had excelled at Oxford, despite his penchant for getting up to all the shenanigans that boys of his background enjoyed at that age. He had managed to find the perfect balance of success and indolence. He could surely understand the words of one young woman who was speaking the same language he had been born to. But he couldn't understand this one.

"Have you run mad, Amelia? Why would your mother mind? Your mother loves me."

"That she does, Viscount Adelaide," Amelia replied pointedly, seeming to imply that he should know exactly what she was on about. When he continued to stare at her as though she had lost her mind, the girl sighed dramatically and explained. "Luce, think about it. We're in London for the Season. In other words, I'm in the Marriage Mart. You are a highly eligible bachelor, whether you're actually interested in matrimony or not. If you were to turn up to take me for a drive, it would put ideas into Mother's head."

"No, it wouldn't," he said with a scoff. "Don't be ridiculous. I've been visiting your family since I was a child. Surely, she would be more bothered if I don't turn up to take you for a drive. In fact, I would argue it's the polite thing to do."

Lucian watched as the girl he had known since she was in pigtails stared at him with the most mature expression he'd ever seen on her face. He felt for a moment as though she were reading his thoughts, and he quailed.

Finally, she nodded. "Perhaps you're right. In any case, even if it gives her ideas, it probably can't be worse than the despair she's suffering over my lack of success."

Before Lucian could demand further explanation, their dance was coming to an end. As she curtsied to him and took her leave, Lucian had to ask himself which dance this qualified as. He had intended to dance with one of each—a Diamond and a Wallflower. He would have classified Amelia as a Diamond, but she assured him she was a wallflower. Could he say he was finished since he had done both at once? The thought was tempting, but it would set tongues to wagging far more than he was willing to endure if he was noted to have only danced with one partner.

With a sigh, he decided the only opinion that mattered was his own, so he would count his friend's sister as the Diamond and seek out a wallflower. But not an awkward one. Not that he would know whether or not she was awkward from appearances. His eyes quickly scanned the assorted guests.

Miss Daisy Alcott would do, he supposed. He had spoken with her at least once or twice and knew she could carry a conversation and didn't giggle excessively. She was another one that seemed not to have taken so well in her debut. And for poor Miss Daisy, it was now her second Season. It was a lucky thing for her that her father's pockets were far from shallow.

Read the entire book today!

Intriguing Lord Adelaide

Also in this series:

Convincing Mr. Northcott

Her reputation is on the line. So is his heart...

About the Author

I learned to read when I was four or five, listening to my mother read to me when I was lonely after my brother started school. Ever since, I've had my head buried in books. I love words – historical plaques, signs, the cereal box – but my first love has always been novels.

A little over ten years ago my husband dared me to write a book instead of always reading them. I didn't think I'd be able to do it, but to my surprise I love writing. Those early efforts eventually became my first published book – Tempting the Earl (published by Avalon Books in 2010). It has been a thrilling adventure as I learned to navigate the world of publishing.

I believe firmly that everyone deserves a happily ever after. I want my readers to be able to escape from the everyday for a little while and feel upbeat and refreshed when they get to the end of my books.

When not reading or writing, I can be found traipsing around my neighbourhood or travelling the world with my favourite companion.

Stay in touch:

Website Facebook Instagram

Stay in touch with Wendy May Andrews
and forthcoming publishing news.

Sign up for her biweekly newsletter
at wendymayandrews.com

Printed in Dunstable, United Kingdom

80634330R00068